"Described as a 'sober farce,' this book is anything but sober. Wild, hilarious, fast moving, irreverent and comic would be the better way to describe it. . . . Not since the publication of Mr. O'Brien's first book, *At Swim-Two-Birds*, has such a comic novel come out of Ireland."
—**Shaun O'Criadin,** *New York Herald Tribune*

"The conversation is a delight—it seems no Irishman can be dull when talking—and the atmosphere of a lower-middle-class family, with its cheerless, shabby, restricted way of life, is well done."—*Library Journal*

"Flann O'Brien's *The Hard Life* is a comic Irish novel that derives its effect from an absolutely deadpan approach, for the narrator is a small boy who, for the better part of the time, has only the foggiest notion of what he is describing. Young Finbarr commands a glorious version of the English language combined with a totally impartial view of adult actions. The two things produce remarkable results."—**Phoebe Adams,** *Atlantic*

"Mixing mild parody with whirlwind farce, O'Brien quickly has Manus (referred to simply as 'The Brother') escape to England and there grow rich by founding a bogus correspondence academy. . . . In The Brother, O'Brien has turned loose a memorably monstrous archetypal entrepreneur."—*Time*

"The dialogue is first-rate, as is the Dublin atmosphere; and some of his characters are as rich and yeasty as good porter foaming out of the jar."—*Times Literary Supplement*

"Mr. O'Brien's almost callous economy of language, combined with an odd moral sensitivity, renders beastliness truly beastly but also completely funny."
—**Simon Raven**

Other Books by Flann O'Brien

Novels

At Swim-Two-Birds
The Third Policeman
The Poor Mouth (An Béal Bocht)
The Dalkey Archive

Collections

At War
The Best of Myles
Stories and Plays
A Flann O'Brien Reader
The Hair of the Dogma
Further Cuttings from Cruiskeen Lawn
Myles Away from Dublin
Myles Before Myles

Flann O'Brien

The Hard Life

An Exegesis of Squalor

Dalkey Archive Press
Normal · London

First Dalkey Archive edition, March 1994
Second printing, September 1996
Third printing, February 2006

Library of Congress Cataloging-in-Publication Data:

O'Brien, Flann, 1911-1966.
    The hard life : an exegesis of squalor / Flann O'Brien. — 1st
Dalkey Archive ed.
        1. Brothers—Ireland—Dublin—Fiction. 2. Orphans—Ireland—
Dublin—Fiction. 3. Dublin (Ireland)—Fiction. I. Title.
PR6029.N56H35   1994   823'.912—dc20   93-21207
ISBN 1-56478-141-0

Partially funded by a grant from the Illinois Arts Council,
a state agency.

Dalkey Archive Press is a nonprofit organization whose mission is
to promote international cultural understanding and provide
a forum for dialogue for the literary arts.

www.dalkeyarchive.com

Printed on permanent/durable acid-free paper, bound in the
United States of America, and distributed throughout
North America and Europe.

I honourably present to

GRAHAM GREENE

whose own forms of gloom I admire,
this misterpiece

All the persons in this book are real
and none is fictitious
even in part

Tout le trouble du monde vient de ce qu'on ne sait pas rester seul dans sa chambre—PASCAL

THE HARD LIFE

1

I<small>T</small> is not that I half knew my mother. I knew half of her: the lower half—her lap, legs, feet, her hands and wrists as she bent forward. Very dimly I seem to remember her voice. At the time, of course, I was very young. Then one day she did not seem to be there any more. So far as I knew she had gone away without a word, no good-bye or good night. A while afterwards I asked my brother, five years my senior, where the mammy was.

—She is gone to a better land, he said.

—Will she be back?

—I don't think so.

—Mean to say we'll never see her again?

—I do think we will. She is staying with the old man.

At the time I found all this very vague and unsatisfying. I had never met my father at all but in due time I was to see and study a faded brown photograph—a stern upright figure wearing great moustaches and attired in a uniform with a large peaked cap. I could never make out what the uniform stood for. He might have been a field marshal or an admiral, or just an orderly officer in the fire brigade; indeed, he might have been a postman.

My memory is a bit mixed about what exactly happened after the mammy went away, but a streel of a girl with long lank fair hair arrived to look after myself and the brother. She did not talk very much and seemed to be in a permanent bad temper. We knew her as Miss Annie. At least that is what she ordered us to call her. She spent a lot of time washing and cooking, specializing in boxty and kalecannon and eternally making mince balls covered with a greasy paste. I got to hate those things.

—If we're ever sent to jail, the brother said one night in bed, we'll be well used to it before we go in. Did you ever see the like of the dinner we're getting? I would say that woman Annie is a bit batty.

—If you mean the mince balls, I said, I think they're all right—if we didn't see so many of them, so often.

—I'm certain they're very bad for us.

—Well, that paste stuff is too thick.

—How well the mammy thought nothing of a bit of ham boiled with cabbage once a week. Remember that?

—I don't. I hadn't any teeth at that time. What's ham?

—Ham? Great stuff, man. It's a class of a red meat that comes from the County Limerick.

That's merely my recollection of the silly sort of conversation we had. Probably it is all wrong.

How long this situation—a sort of interregnum, lacuna or hiatus—lasted I cannot say, but I do remember that when myself and the brother noticed that Miss Annie was washing more savagely, mangling and ironing almost with ferocity, and *packing*, we knew something was afoot. And we were not mistaken.

One morning after breakfast (stirabout and tea with bread and jam) a cab arrived and out of it came a very strange elderly lady on a stick. I saw her first through the window. Her hair peeping from under her hat was grey, her face very red, and she walked slowly as if her sight was bad. Miss Annie let her in, first telling us that here was Mrs. Crotty and to be good. She stood in silence for a moment in the kitchen, staring rather blankly about her.

—These are the two rascals, Mrs. Crotty, Miss Annie said.

—And very well they're looking, God bless them, Mrs. Crotty said in a high voice. Do they do everything they're told?

—Oh, I suppose they do, but sometimes it's a job to make them take their milk.

—Well faith now, Mrs. Crotty said in a shocked tone, did you ever hear of such nonsense? When I was their age I could never get *enough* milk. Never. I could drink jugs of it. Buttermilk too. Nothing in the wide world is better for the stomach or the nerves. Night and day I am telling Mr. Collopy that but you might as well be talking to *that table!*

Here she struck the table with her stick. Miss Annie looked startled that her trivial mention of milk should induce such emphasis. She took off her apron.

—We'll see, she said ominously. Is the cabby outside? I have all the stuff ready in there.

—Yes, Mr. Hanafin is out there. Just call him in. Are these young gentlemen washed?

—As far as possible. What the pair of them need is a good bath. You know the way the water is here.

—The Lord save us, Mrs. Crotty said grimacing, is there anything under heaven's sky more terrible than dirt. But sure we'll see after all that in good time, please God. Well now!

Miss Annie went out and came back with Mr. Hanafin the cabby. He had a ruby face, maybe from

all the porter he drank, and was correctly dressed—
hard hat and a caped surcoat of dark green.

—The top of the morning to you all, he said
genially. I was just saying, Mrs. Crotty, that Miss
Annie is looking very well.

—Is that so? Well, she had a bit of a handful here
but then Mr. Collopy is another handful and maybe
a little rest from him was as good to her as a fortnight in Skerries.

—Ah now, she has great colour, Mr. Hanafin replied pleasantly. Is them two young archdukes to be
me passengers?

—Yes, Miss Annie said, they are the main cargo.
See you don't spill them out.

—Be the dad, Mr. Hanafin said smiling, Marius
will be delighted. We'll get a right trot this morning.

—Who is Marius? the brother asked.

—The mare, man.

Afterwards the brother told me he thought this
was a strange name for a mare. Maria would have
been better. He was a very wide-awake character
even then. I think I used some coarse word here
about the animal outside. He told me I should not
speak like that.

—Why?

—Teresa would not like it.

—Who is Teresa?

—Our sister.

—Our *sister*? WHAT?

Mrs. Crotty told Miss Annie to show Mr. Hanafin where the baggage was, and she led him into the back room off the kitchen. There was a lot of noisy fumbling and pulling. The bulk of the baggage could only be explained by having blankets and pillows and other bedclothes tied up, for the wardrobe of the brother and myself was not . . . well . . . extensive. Perhaps there were curtains there, too.

At last Mr. Hanafin had everything packed away on the roof of the cab. It was summer and the brother and I travelled as we stood. Miss Annie carefully locked the house and she and Mrs. Crotty stowed themselves fastidiously in the back seat of the cab, ourselves sitting facing them. The journey was enjoyable, great houses sliding past, trams clanging in the middle of the road, large thickly made horses hauling heavy drays, and our own Marius making delightful music with her hooves. As I was later to know, our destination was Warrington Place, a rather junior continuation of lordly Herbert Place along the canal on the south side of the great city of Dublin.

Reckoning backwards, I find I was about five years old. The year was 1890, and my young bones told me that a great change was coming in my life. Little did I know just then how big the change. I was about to meet Mr. Collopy.

2

T HERE is something misleading but not dishonest in this portrait of Mr. Collopy. It cannot be truly my impression of him when I first saw him but rather a synthesis of all the thoughts and experiences I had of him over the years, a long look backwards. But I do remember clearly enough that my first glimpse of him was, so to speak, his absence: Mrs. Crotty, having knocked imperiously on the door, immediately began rooting in her handbag for the key. It was plain she did not expect the door to be opened.

—There is a clap of rain coming, she remarked to Miss Annie.

—Seemingly, Miss Annie said.

Mrs. Crotty opened the door and led us in single file into the front kitchen, semi-basement, Mr. Hanafin bringing up the rear with some bags.

He was sitting there at the range in a crooked, collapsed sort of cane armchair, small reddish eyes looking up at us over the rims of steel spectacles, the head bent forward for closer scrutiny. Over an ample crown, long grey hair was plastered in a tattered way. The whole mouth region was concealed by a great untidy dark brush of a moustache, discoloured at the edges, and a fading chin was joined to a stringy neck which disappeared into a white celluloid collar with no tie. Nondescript clothes contained a meagre frame of low stature and the feet wore large boots with the laces undone.

—Heavenly fathers, he said in a flat voice, but you are very early. Morning, Hanafin.

—Morra, Mr. Collopy, Mr. Hanafin said.

—Annie here had everything infastatiously in order, Mrs. Crotty said, thanks be to God.

—I wonder now, Miss Annie said.

—Troth, Mr. Collopy, Mr. Hanafin beamed, but I never seen you looking better. You have a right bit of colour up whatever you are doing with yourself at all.

The brother and myself looked at Mr. Collopy's slack grey face and then looked at each other.

—Well the dear knows, Mr. Collopy said, I don't think hard work ever hurt anybody. Put that stuff in the back room for the present, Hanafin. Well now, Mrs. Crotty, are these the two pishrogues out of the storm? They are not getting any thinner from the good dinners you have been putting into them, Annie, and that's a fact.

—Seemingly, Miss Annie said.

—Pray introduce me, if you please, Mrs. Crotty.

We went forward and had our names recited. Without rising, Mr. Collopy made good an undone button at the neck of the brother's jersey and then shook hands with us solemnly. From his waistcoat he extracted two pennies and presented one to each of us.

—I cross your hands with earthly goods, he said, and at the same time I put my blessing on your souls.

—Thanks for the earthly goods, the brother said.

—Manus and Finbarr are fine names, fine Irish names, Mr. Collopy said. In the Latin Manus means big. Remember that. Ecce Sacerdos Manus comes into the Missal, and that Manus is such an uplifting name. Ah but Finbarr is the real Irish, for he was a saint from the County Cork. Far and wide he spread the Gospel thousands of years ago for all the thanks he got, for I believe he died of starvation at the heel of the hunt on some island on the river Lee, down fornenst Queenstown.

—I always heard that Saint Finbarr was a Protestant, Mrs. Crotty snapped. Dug with the other foot. God knows what put it into the head of anybody to put a name the like of that on the poor bookul.

—Nonsense, Mrs. Crotty. His heart was to Ireland and his soul to the Bishop of Rome. What is sticking out of that bag, Hanafin? Are they brooms or shovels or what?

Mr. Hanafin had reappeared with a new load of baggage and followed Mr. Collopy's gaze to one item.

—Faith now, Mr. Collopy, he replied, and damn the shovels. They are hurling sticks. Best of Irish ash and from the County Kilkenny, I'll go bail.

—I am delighted to hear it. From the winding banks of Nore, ah? Many a good puck I had myself in the quondam days of my nonage. I could draw on a ball in those days and clatter in a goal from midfield, man.

—Well, it's no wonder you are never done talking about the rheumatism in your knuckles, Mrs. Crotty said bleakly.

—That will do you, Mrs. Crotty. It was a fine manly game and I am not ashamed of any wounds I may still carry. In those days you were damn nothing if you weren't a hurler. Cardinal Logue is a hurler and a native Irish speaker, revered by Pope and man. Were *you* a hurler, Hanafin?

—In my part of the country—Tinahely—we went in for the football.

—Michael Cusack's Gaelic code, I hope?

—Oh, certaintly, Mr. Collopy.

—That's good. The native games for the native people. By dad and I see young thullabawns of fellows got out in baggy drawers playing this new golf out beyond on the Bull Island. For pity's sake sure that isn't a game at all.

—Oh, you'll always find the fashionable jackeen in Dublin and that's a certainty, Mr. Hanafin said. They'd wear nightshirts if they seen the British military playing polo in nightshirts above in the park. Damn the bit of shame they have.

—And then you have all this talk about Home Rule, Mr. Collopy asserted. Well how are you! We're as fit for Home Rule here as the blue men in Africa if we are to judge by those Bull Island looderamawns.

—Sit over here at the table, Mrs. Crotty said. Is that tea drawn, Annie?

—Seemingly, Miss Annie said.

We all sat down and Mr. Hanafin departed, leaving a shower of blessings on us.

It is seemly for me to explain here, I feel, the nature and standing of the persons present. Mr. Collopy was my mother's half-brother and was therefore my own half-uncle. He had married twice, Miss Annie being his daughter by his first marriage. Mrs. Crotty was his second wife but she was never called Mrs. Collopy, why I cannot say. She may have deliberately retained the name of her first husband in loving memory of him or the habit may have grown up through the absence of mind. Moreover, she always called her second husband by the formal style of Mr. Collopy as he also called her Mrs. Crotty, at least in the presence of other parties; I cannot speak for what usage obtained in private. An ill-disposed person might suspect that they were not married at all and that Mrs. Crotty was a kept woman or resident prostitute. But that is quite unthinkable, if only because of Mr. Collopy's close interest in the Church and in matters of doctrine and dogma, and also his long friendship with the German priest from Leeson Street, Father Kurt Fahrt, S.J., who was a frequent caller.

It is seemly, as I have said, to give that explanation but I cannot pretend to have illuminated the situation or made it more reasonable.

3

THE years passed slowly in this household where the atmosphere could be described as a dead one. The brother, five years older than myself, was first to be sent to school, being marched off early one morning by Mr. Collopy to see the Superior of the Christian Brothers' school at Westland Row. A person might think the occasion was one merely of formal introduction and enrolment, but when Mr. Collopy returned, he was alone.

—By God's will, he explained, Manus's foot has been placed today on the first rung of the ladder of learning and achievement, and on yonder pinnacle beckons the lone star.

—The unfortunate boy had no lunch, Mrs. Crotty said in a shrill voice.

—You might consider, Mrs. Crotty, that the Lord would provide, even as He does for the birds of the air. I gave the bosthoon a tuppence. Brother Cruppy told me that the boys can get a right bag of broken biscuits for a penny in a barber's shop there up the lane.

—And what about milk?

—Are you out of your wits, woman? You know the gorawars you have to get him to drink his milk in this kitchen. He thinks milk is poison, the same way *you* think a drop of malt is poison. That reminds me—I think I deserve a smahan. Where's my crock?

The brother, who had become more secretive as time went on, did not confide much in me about his new station except that "school was a bugger." Sooner than I thought, my own turn was to come. One evening Mr. Collopy asked me where the morning paper was. I handed him the nearest I could find. He handed it back to me.

—This morning's I told you.

—I think that's this morning's.

—You *think*? Can you not read, boy?

—Well . . . no.

—Well, may the sweet Almighty God look down on us with compassion! Do you realize that at your age Mose Art had written four symphonies and any God's amount of lovely songs? Pagan Neeny had given a recital on the fiddle before the King of Prussia and John the Baptist was stranded in the desert with damn the thing to eat only locusts and wild honey. Have you no shame, man?

—Well, I'm young yet.

—Is that a fact now? You are like the rest of them, you are counting from the wrong end. How do you know you are not within three months of the end of your life?

—Oh my God!

—Hah?

—But——

—You may put your buts back in your pocket. I will tell you what you'll do. You'll get up tomorrow morning at the stroke of eight o'clock and you will give yourself a good wash for yourself.

That night the brother said in bed, not without glee, that somehow he thought I would soon be master of Latin and Shakespeare and that Brother Cruppy would shower heavenly bread on me with his class in Christian Doctrine and give me some idea of what the early Christians went through in the arena by thrashing the life out of me. Unhappy was the eye I closed that night. But the brother was only partly right. To my surprise, Mr. Collopy next morning led me at a smart pace up the bank of the

canal, penetrated to Synge Street and rang the bell
at the residential part of the Christian Brothers'
establishment there. When a slatternly young man
in black answered, Mr. Collopy said he wanted to
see the Superior, Brother Gaskett. We were shown
into a gaunt little room which had on the wall a
steel engraving of the head of Brother Rice, founder
of the Order, a few chairs and a table—nothing
more.

—They say piety has a smell, Mr. Collopy mused,
half to himself. It's a perverse notion. What they
mean is only the absence of the smell of women.

He looked at me.

—Did you know that no living woman is allowed
into this holy house? That is as it should be. Even
if a Brother has to see his own mother, he has to
meet her in secret below at the Imperial Hotel.
What do you think of that?

—I think it is very hard, I said. Couldn't she call
to see him here and have another Brother present,
like they do in jails when there is a warder present
on visiting day?

—Well, that's the queer comparison, I'll warrant.
Indeed, this house may be a jail of a kind but the
chains are of purest eighteen-carat finest gold which
the holy Brothers like to kiss on their bended knees.

The door opened silently and an elderly stout
man with a sad face glided in. He smiled primly and
gave us an odd handshake, keeping his elbow bent
and holding the extended hand against his breast.

—Isn't that the lovely morning, Mr. Collopy, he said hoarsely.

—It is, thank God, Brother Gaskett, Mr. Collopy replied as we all sat down. Need I tell you why I brought this young ruffian along?

—Well, it wasn't to teach him how to play cards.

—You are right there, Brother. His name is Finbarr.

—Well now, look at that! That is a beautiful name, one that is honoured by the Church. I presume you would like us to try to extend Finbarr's knowledge?

—That is a nice way of putting it, Brother Gaskett. I think they will have to be very big extensions because damn the thing he knows but low songs from the pantomimes, come-all-ye's by Cathal McGarvey, and his prayers. I suppose you'll take him in, Brother?

—Of course I will. Certainly, I will teach him everything from the three Rs to Euclid and Aristophanes and the tongue of the Gael. We will give him a thorough grounding in the Faith and, with God's help, if one day he should feel like joining the Order, there will always be a place for him in this humble establishment. After he has been trained, of course.

The tail-end of that speech certainly startled me, even to tempting me to put in some sort of caveat. I did not like it even as a joke, nor the greasy Brother making it.

—I . . . I think that could wait a bit, Brother Gaskett, I stammered.

He laughed mirthlessly.

—Ah but of course, Finbarr. One thing at a time.

Then he and Mr. Collopy indulged in some muttered consultation jaw to jaw, and the latter got up to leave. I also rose but he made a gesture.

—We'll stay where we are now, he said. Brother Gaskett thinks you might start right away. Always better to take the bull by the horns.

Though not quite unexpected, this rather shocked me.

—But, I said in a loud voice, I had no lunch . . . no broken biscuits.

—Never mind, Brother Gaskett said, we will give you a half-day to begin with.

That is how I entered the sinister portals of Synge Street School. Soon I was to get to know the instrument known as "the leather." It is not, as one would imagine, a strap of the kind used on bags. It is a number of such straps sewn together to form a thing of great thickness that is nearly as rigid as a club but just sufficiently flexible to prevent the breaking of the bones of the hand. Blows of it, particularly if directed (as often they deliberately were) to the top of the thumb or wrist, conferred immediate paralysis followed by agony as the blood tried to get back to the afflicted part. Later I was to learn from the brother a certain routine of prophylaxis he had devised but it worked only partly.

Neither of us found out what Mr. Collopy's reason was for sending us to different schools. The brother thought it was to prevent us "cogging," or copying each other's home exercises, of which we were given an immense programme to get through every night. This was scarcely correct, for an elaborate system for "cogging" already existed in each school itself, for those who arrived early in the morning. My own feeling was that the move was prompted by Mr. Collopy's innate craftiness and the general principle of *divide et impera*.

4

AND still the years kept rolling on, and uneventfully enough, thank God. I was now about eleven, the brother sixteen and convinced he was a fully grown man.

One day in spring about half three I was trudging wearily home from school at Synge Street. I was on the remote or canal side of the roadway near home. I happened to glance up at the house when about fifty yards away and, turned to cold stone, stopped dead in my tracks. My heart thumped wildly against my ribs and my eyes fell to the ground. I blessed myself. Timidly I looked up again. Yes!

To the left of the house entrance and perhaps fifteen yards from it a tallish tree stood in the front garden. Head and shoulders above the tree but not quite near it was the brother. I stared at the apparition in the manner fascinated animals are reputed to stare at deadly snakes about to strike. He began waving his arms in a sickening way, and the next prospect I had of him was his back. He was returning towards the house *and he was walking on air*! Now thoroughly scared, I thought of Another who had walked on water. I again looked away helplessly, and after a little time painfully stumbled into the house. I must have looked very pale but went in and said nothing.

Mr. Collopy was not in his usual chair at the range. Annie—we had now learned to drop the "Miss"—placed potatoes and a big plate of stew before me. I thought it would be well to affect a casual manner.

—Where's Mr. Collopy? I asked.

She nodded towards the back room.

—He's inside, she said. I don't know what Father's at. He's in there with a tape taking measurements. I'm afraid poor Mrs. Crotty's getting worse. She had Dr. Blennerhassett again this morning. God look down on us all!

Mrs. Crotty was certainly sick. She had taken to the bed two months before and insisted that the door between her bedroom and the kitchen should be always left slightly ajar so that her cries, often faint, could be heard either by Mr. Collopy or Annie. Neither myself nor the brother ever entered the room but all the same I had accidentally seen her on several occasions. This was when she was coming down the stairs leaning on Mr. Collopy and clutching the banister with one frail hand, her robe or nightdress of fantastic shape and colour and a frightening pallor on her spent face.

—I'm afraid she *is* pretty sick, I said.

—Seemingly.

I finished with a cup of tea, then casually left the kitchen and went upstairs, my heart again making its excitement known. I entered the bedroom.

The brother, his back to me, was bending over a table examining some small metal objects. He looked up and nodded abstractedly.

—Do you mind, I said nervously, do you mind answering a question?

—What question? I have got a great bit of gear here.

—Listen to the question. When I was coming in a while back, did I see you walking on the air?

.He turned again to stare at me and then laughed loudly.

—Well by damn, he chuckled, I suppose you did, in a manner of speaking.

—What do you mean?

—Your question is interesting. Tell me: did it look well?

—If you want to know, it looked unnatural and if you are taking advantage of a power not of God, if you are dealing in godless things of darkness, I would strongly advise you to see Father Fahrt, because these things will lead to no good.

Here he sniggered.

—Have a look out of the window, he said.

I went and did so very gingerly. Between the sill and a stout branch near the top of the tree stretched a very taut wire, which I now saw came in at the base of the closed window and was anchored with some tightening device to the leg of the bed, which was in against the wall.

—My God Almighty! I exclaimed.

—Isn't it good?

—A bloody wire-walker, by cripes!

—I got the stuff from Jem out of the Queen's. There's nothing at all to it. If I rigged the wire across this room tomorrow and only a foot from the floor, you'd walk it yourself with very little practice. What's the difference? What's the difference if you're an inch or a mile up? The only trouble is what they call psychological. It's a new word but I know what it means. The balancing part of it is child's play, and the trick is to put all idea of height out of your mind. It *looks* dangerous, of course, but there's money in that sort of danger. Safe danger.

—What happens if you fall and break your neck?

—Did you ever hear of Blondin? He died in his bed at the age of seventy-three, and fifty years ago he walked on a wire across Niagara Falls, one hundred and sixty feet above the roaring water. And several times—carrying a man on his back, stopping to fry eggs, a great man altogether. And didn't he appear once in Belfast?

—I think you are going off your head.

—I'm going to make money, for I have . . . certain schemes, certain very important schemes. Look what I have here. A printing machine. I got it from one of the lads at Westland Row, who stole it from his uncle. It's simple to operate, though it's old.

But I could not detach my mind from that wire.

—So you're to be the Blondin of Dublin?

—Well, why not?

—Niagara is too far away, of course. I suppose you'll sling a wire over the Liffey?

He started, threw down some metal thing, and turned to me wide-eyed.

—Well sweet God, he said, you have certainly said something. *You have certainly said something.* Sling a wire over the Liffey? The Masked Daredevil from Mount Street! There's a fortune there—*a fortune!* Lord save us, why didn't I think of it?

—I was only joking, for goodness' sake.

—*Joking?* I hope you'll keep on joking like that. I'll see Father Fahrt about this.

—To bless you before you risk your life?

—Balls! I'll need an organizer, a manager. Father

Fahrt knows a lot of those young teachers and I'll get him to put me on to one of them. They're a sporty crowd. Do you remember Frank Corkey, N.T.? He was in this house once, a spoilt Jesuit. That man would blow up the walls of Jerusalem for two quid. He'd be the very man.

—And get sacked from his school for helping a young madman to kill himself?

—I'll get him. You wait and see.

That ended that day's surprising disputation. I was secretly amused at the idea of the brother getting on to Father Fahrt about organizing a walk across the Liffey on a tight-wire, with Mr. Collopy sprawled in his cane armchair a few feet away listening to the appeal. I had heard of earthquakes and the devastation attending them. Here surely would be a terrible upheaval.

But once more I reckoned without the brother. Without saying a word he slipped off one day up to 35 Lower Leeson Street and saw Father Fahrt privately. He said so when he returned that evening, looking slightly daunted.

—The holy friar, he said, won't hear of it. Asked did I think I was a cornerboy or had I no respect for my family. Public pranks is what he called walking the high wire. Threatened to tell ould Collopy if I didn't put the idea out of my head. Asked me to promise. I promised, of course. But I'll find Corkey on my own and we'll make a damn fine day of it, believe you me. Had I no respect for my family, ah? What family?

—No Jesuit likes being mistaken for a Barnum, I pointed out.

Rather bitterly he said: You'll hear more about this.

I felt sure I would.

5

I T had become evident to me that one of the brother's schemes was in operation, for a considerable stream of letters addressed to him began to arrive at the house, and he had become more secretive than ever. I refused to give him the satisfaction of asking him what he had been up to. I will tell all about that later but just now I wish to give an account of the sort of evening we had in our kitchen, not once but very many times, and the type of talk that went on. As usual, the subject under discussion was never named.

The brother and myself were at the table, struggling through that wretched homework, cursing Wordsworth and Euclid and Christian Doctrine and all similar scourges of youth. Mr. Collopy was slumped in his cane armchair, the steel-rimmed glasses far down his nose. In an easy chair opposite was Father Kurt Fahrt who was a very tall man, thin, ascetic, grey-haired, blue about the jaws, with a neck so slender that there would be room, so to speak, for two of them inside his priestly collar. On the edge of the range, handy to the reach of those philosophers, was a glass. On the floor beside Mr. Collopy's chair was what was known as "the crock." It was in fact a squat earthenware container, having an ear on each side, in which the Kilbeggan Distillery marketed its wares. The Irish words for whiskey—*Uisge Beatha*—were burnt into its face. This vessel was, of course, opaque and therefore mysterious; one could not tell how empty or full it was, nor how much Mr. Collopy had been drinking. The door of Mrs. Crotty's bedroom was, as usual, very slightly ajar.

—What the devil ails you, Father? Mr. Collopy asked almost irritably.

—Oh, it's nothing much, Collopy, Father Fahrt said.

—But heavens above, this scrabbling and scratching——

—Forgive me. I have a touch of psoriasis about the back and chest.

—The sore *what*?

—Psoriasis. A little skin ailment.

—Lord save us, I thought you said you had sore eyes. Is there any question of scabs or that class of thing?

—Oh, not at all. I am taking treatment. An ointment containing stuff known as chrysarobin.

—Well, this sore-whatever-it-is causes itching?

Father Fahrt laughed softly.

—Sometimes it feels more like etching, he smiled.

—The man for that is sulphur. Sulphur is one of the great sovereign remedies of the world. Bedamn but a friend of mine uses a lot of sulphur even in his garden.

Here Father Fahrt unconsciously scratched himself.

—Let us forget about such trivial things, he said, and thank God it is not something serious. So, Collopy, you're getting worked up again about your plan?

—It's a shame, Father, Mr. Collopy said warmly. It's a bloody shame and that's what it is.

—Well, Collopy, what are we for in this world? We are here to suffer. We must sanctify ourselves. That's what suffering is for.

—Do you know, Father, Mr. Collopy said testily, I am getting a bit sick in my intesteens at all this talk of yours about suffering. You seem to be very fond of suffering when other people do it. What would you do if you had the same situation in your own house?

—In my own house I would do what my Superior instructs me to do. My Order is really an army. We are under orders.

—Give me your glass, your Holiness.

—Not much now, Collopy.

There was a small silence here that seemed portentous, though I did not raise my head to look.

—Father, said Mr. Collopy at last, you would go off your bloody head if you had the same situation in your own house. You would make a show of yourself. You would tell Father Superior to go to hell, lep out the front door and bugger off down to Stephen's Green. Oh, I'm up to ye saints. Well up to ye. Do you not think that women have enough suffering, as you call it, bringing babbies into the world? And why do they do that? Is it because they're mad to sanctify themselves? Well faith no! It's because the husband is one great torch ablaze with the fires of lust!

—Collopy, please, Father Fahrt said in mild remonstrance. That attitude is quite wrong. Procreation is the *right* of a married man. Indeed it is his duty for the greater glory of God. It is a duty enjoined by the sacrament of marriage.

—Oh is that so, Mr. Collopy said loudly, is that so indeed. To bring unfortunate new bosthoons into this vale of tears for more of this suffering of yours, ah? Another woman maybe. Sweet Lord!

—Now, now, Collopy.

—Tell me this, Father. Would you say it's *natural* for a woman to have children?

—Provided she is married in a union blessed by the Church—yes. Most natural and most desirable. It is a holy thing to raise children to the greater glory of God. Your catechism will tell you that. The celibate and priestly state is the holiest of all but the station of the married man is not ignoble. And of course the modest married woman is the handmaid of the Lord.

—Very good, Mr. Collopy said warmly. Then tell me this. Is the other business natural?

—Certainly. Our bodies are sacred temples. It is a function.

—Very well. What name have you for the dirty ignoramuses who more or less ban that function?

—It is, ah, thoughtlessness, Father Fahrt said in his mildest voice. Perhaps if a strong hint were dropped . . .

—*If a hint were dropped*, Mr. Collopy exploded. *If a hint were dropped!* Well the dear knows I think you are trying to destroy my temper, Father, and put me out of my wits and make an unfortunate shaughraun out of me. If a hint were dropped, my hat and parsley! Right well you know that I have the trotters wore off me going up the stairs of that filthy Corporation begging them, telling them, ordering them to do something. I have shown you copies of the letters I have sent to that booby the Lord Mayor. That's one man that knows all about chains, anyhow. What result have I got? Nothing at all but abuse from cornerboys and jacks in office.

—Has it ever entered your head, Collopy, that perhaps you are not the most tactful of men?

—Tact, is it? Is that the latest? Give me your glass.

Another pause for decantation and recollection.

—What I would like to do, Mr. Collopy said sententiously, is write and publish a long storybook about your theories in favour of suffering. Damn the thing you know about suffering yourself. Only people of no experience have theories. Of course you are only spewing out what you were taught in the holy schools. "By the sweat of thy brow shalt thou mourn." Oh, the grand old Catholic Church has always had great praise for sufferers.

—That phrase you quoted was inaccurate, Collopy.

—Well, am I supposed to be a deacon or a Bible scholar or what? You won't find Quakers or swaddlers coming out with any of this guff about suffering. They treat their employees right, they have proper accommodation for them, they know how to make plenty of money honestly and they are as holy —every man-jack of them—as any blooming Jesuit or the Pope of Rome himself.

—Let us leave the Holy Father out of this dispute, whatever about humble members of my Society, Father Fahrt said piously.

Suddenly he scratched himself earnestly.

—Did I hear you right when you said "humble," Father? An humble Jesuit would be like a dog without a tail or a woman without a knickers on her. Did you ever hear tell of the Spanish Inquisition?

—I did, of course, Father Fahrt said unperturbed. The faith was in danger in Spain. If a bad wind will blow out your candle, you will protect your candle with the shade of your hand. Or perhaps some sort of cardboard shield.

—Cardboard shield? Mr. Collopy echoed scornfully. Well, damn the cardboard shields the Dominicans used in Spain, those bloodstained bowsies.

—My own Order, Father Fahrt said modestly, was under the thumb of the Suprema in Madrid and yet I make no complaint.

—Well, isn't that very good of you, Father? Your own Order was kicked about by those barbarian hooligans in the cowls and *you* make no complaint, sitting there with a glass of malt in your hand. Faith but you're the modest, dacent man, God bless you.

—I merely meant, Collopy, that in a scheme to eradicate serious evil, sometimes we must all suffer.

—And what's wrong with that, Father? Isn't suffering grand?

—It is not pleasant but it is salutary.

—You have a smart answer for everything. "Do you believe in the true faith?" "No." "Very well. Eight hundred lashes." If that's the Catholic Church for you, is it any wonder there was a Reformation? Three cheers for Martin Luther!

Father Fahrt was shocked.

—Collopy, please remember that you belong to the true fold yourself. That talk is scandalous.

—True fold? Do I? And doesn't the Lord Mayor
and the other gougers in the City Hall? And look at
the way they're behaving—*killing* unfortunate
women.

—Never mind that subject.

—Till the day I die I'll mind that subject, Mr.
Collopy retorted excitedly. Eight hundred lashes
for telling the truth according to your conscience?
What am I talking about—the holy friars in Spain
propagated the true faith by driving red-hot nails
into the backs of unfortunate Jewmen.

—Nonsense.

—And scalding their testicles with boiling water.

—You exaggerate, Collopy.

—And ramming barbed wire or something of the
kind up where-you-know. And all A.M.D.G., to use
your own motto, Father.

—For heaven's sake, Collopy, have sense, Father
Fahrt said calmly and sadly. I do not know where
you have read those lurid and silly things.

—Father Fahrt, Mr. Collopy said earnestly, you
don't like the Reformation. Maybe I'm not too
fond of it myself, either. But it was our own crowd,
those ruffians in Spain and all, who provoked it.
They called decent men heretics and the remedy
was to put a match to them. To say nothing of a lot
of crooked Popes with their armies and their papal
states, putting duchesses and nuns up the pole and
having all Italy littered with their bastards, and up
to nothing but backstairs work and corruption at

the courts of God knows how many decent foreign kings. Isn't that a fact?

—It is not a fact, Collopy. The Reformation was a doctrinal revolt, inspired I have no doubt by Satan. It had nothing to do with human temporal weaknesses in the Papacy or elsewhere.

—Well now, do you tell me, Mr. Collopy sneered.

—Yes, I do. I hate no man, not even Luther. Indeed, by his translation of the Bible, he can take credit for having in effect invented my own language, *die schöne deutsche Sprache.* But he was possessed by the Devil. He was a heretic. Heresiarch would be a better word. And when he died in 1545——

—Excuse me, Father Fahrt.

I was profoundly startled to hear the brother interjecting. He had been undisguisedly following this heated colloquy but it seemed to me unthinkable and provocative that he should intervene. Clearly Mr. Collopy and Father Fahrt were equally surprised as they swung round their necks to look at him.

—Yes, my lad? Father Fahrt said.

—Luther did not die in 1545, said the brother. It was 1546.

—Well, well, now, maybe you are right, Father Fahrt said good-humouredly. Maybe you are right. Alas, my old head was never very good for figures. Well, Collopy, I see you have a theologian in the family.

—An historian, the brother said.

—And I'll correct that correction, Mr. Collopy said acidly. A bloody young gurrier that won't apply himself with application to his studies, that's what we have. Give me that glass of yours, Father.

There was another intermission while the brother with great elaboration of manner reapplied himself to his studies. After taking a long draught from his new drink, Mr. Collopy sank farther back in his shapeless chair and sighed very deeply.

—I'm afraid, Father Fahrt, he said at last, we are only wasting time and just annoying each other with these arguments. These things have been argued out years ago. You'd imagine we here were like Our Lord disputing with the doctors in the temple. The real question is this: What action can we take? *What can be done?*

—Well, that's certainly a more reasonable approach, Collopy. Much more reasonable. And much more practical.

—*Quod faciamemus,* ah?

—Have you thought about a public meeting at all?

—By the jappers I have, many a time, Mr. Collopy said with some sadness. I gave it my best considerations. It would be no good. And do you know why? Only men go to public meetings. No lady would be found dead at a public meeting. You know that? You would find only prostitutes hanging around. And men? What good are *they?* Sure they don't give a goddam if women were dying like

flies in the streets. They have only two uses for
women, Father—either go to bed with them or else
thrash the life out of them. I was half thinking of
trying to enlist the support of this new Gaelic
League, but I'm afraid they're nothing only a crowd
of thooleramawns. They wouldn't understand this
crisis in our national life. They would think I was
a dirty old man and send for the D.M.P.

—Um.

Father Fahrt frowned speculatively.

—What about making a move at Dublin Castle?
They could certainly put pressure on the Corporation.

—And get myself locked up? I am not a damned
fool.

—Ah! With politics I am not familiar.

—I'm buggered if I can see what's political about
this but those ruffians in the Castle will arrest an
Irishman and charge him with treason if his trousers
are a bit baggy or he forgot to shave. But here's an
approach that came into my head . . .

—What is that, Collopy?

—Why not have the whole scandalous situation
denounced from the pulpit?

—Oh . . . dear.

Father Fahrt gave a low, melodious, sardonic
laugh.

—The Church's first concern, Collopy, is with
faith and morals. Their application to everyday life
is pretty wide but I fear your particular problem is
far, far outside the pale. We couldn't possibly raise

such a matter in a church. It might even give
scandal. If I were to start forth on the subject in
University Church, I think I know what Father
Superior would say, not to mention his Grace the
Archbishop.

—But, look here——

—No, no, now, Collopy. *Ecclesia locuta, causa
finita est.*

—Ah well, that's the way, I suppose, Mr. Collopy
said with tired resignation. The Church keeps very
far from the people in their daily troubles and
travail, but by gob it wasn't like that when we had
the Penal Laws, with Paddy Whack keeping a look-
out for the soldiery from the top of the ditch on a
Sunday morning and the poor pishrogues of peas-
ants below in their rags answering the Hail Mary in
Irish. 'Tis too grand you are getting, Father, yourself and your Church.

—I'm afraid there is such a thing as Canon Law,
Collopy.

—We have too much law in this country. I even
thought of getting in touch with the Freemasons.

—I hope not. It is sinful to have any truck with
those people. They despise the Holy Spirit.

—I doubt if they despise women as much as the
damned Lord Mayor and his Corporation do.

—There is one remedy I am sure you haven't
tried, Collopy.

Here Father Fahrt urgently scratched again.

—I'm sure there is. Probably thousands. What's
the one remedy?

—Prayer.

—The what was that?

—*Prayer.*

—Prayer? I see. You'd never know, we might try that yet. You can move mountains with prayer, I believe, but I'm not trying to move mountains. I'm trying to put a bumb under that Lord Mayor. But there is one very far-fetched idea I've had and damned if I know would it work. I'd want influence . . . a word in high places . . . great tact and plawmaus . . . perhaps a word of support from his Grace. Indeed it might be a complete and final solution to the whole terrible crux. If it came off I would go on a pilgrimage to Lough Derg in thanksgiving.

—It must be a miracle you're looking for if you'd go that far, Collopy, Father Fahrt said smiling. And what is this idea of yours?

—Trams, Father. *Trams.* I don't know how many distinct routes we have here in the city, but say the total is eight. One tram for each route in each direction would suffice, or sixteen trams in all. Old trams repaired and redecorated would do.

—Are you serious, Collopy? Trams?

—Yes, trams. They would have to be distinctive, painted black all over, preferably, and only one sign up front and rear—just the one word WOMEN. Understand? It would be as much as a man's life was worth to try to get into one of them.

—Well, well. At least this idea is novel. Would there be a charge?

—Very likely there would be a penny fare at the beginning. To look for a free service at the start, that would be idealism. But once we have the cars running, we could start an agitation for the wiping out of the penny fare in the interest of humanity.

—I see.

—I would like you to think this thing over, Father. Let us say that a lady and gentleman are walking down the street and have a mind to go for a stroll in the Phoenix Park. Fair enough. But first one thing has to be attended to. They wait at a tram stop. Lo and behold, along comes the Black Tram. The lady steps on board and away she goes on her own. And the whole beauty of the plan is this: *she can get an ordinary tram back* to rejoin her waiting friend. Do you twig?

—Yes, I think I understand.

—Ah, Father, you don't know how dear to my heart this struggle is and the peace that will come down on top of my head when it is happily ended for ever. Decent people should look after women —isn't that right? The weaker sex. Didn't God make them the same as he made you and me, Father?

—He surely did.

—Then why don't we give them fair play? Mean to say, you or I can walk into a pub——

—I *beg* your pardon, Collopy. I certainly can *not* walk into a public house. You never saw a priest in a public house in your life.

—Well, I can walk into a pub and indeed I often do.

—Well, well, Collopy, you are full of ideas but I must be moving. I didn't realize the hour.

—Good enough, but you will call again. Think about what I've said. Can I offer you a final glasheen for the road?

—No thanks indeed, Collopy. Good night now, lads, and mind the Greek article haw-hee-taw.

In unison:

—Good night, Father Fahrt.

He went out with dignity, Mr. Collopy his escort.

6

I T had been a dull autumn day and in the early evening I decided that the weather would make it worth while looking for roach in the canal. My rod was crude enough but I had hooks of a special size which I had put away in a drawer in the bedroom. I got out the rod and went up for a hook. To my surprise the drawer was littered with sixpenny postal orders and also envelopes addressed to the brother describing him as "Director, General Georama Gymnasium." I decided to leave this strange stuff alone, took a hook and went off up along the canal. Perhaps my bait was wrong but I caught nothing and was back home in about an hour. The brother was in the bedroom when I returned, busy writing at the smaller table.

—I was out looking for roach, I remarked, and had to get a hook in that drawer. I see it's full of sixpenny postal orders.

—Not full, he said genially. There are only twenty-eight. But keep that under your hat.

—Twenty-eight is fourteen bob.

—Yes, but I expect a good few more.

—What's all this about General Georama Gymnasium?

—Well, it's my name for the moment, he said.

—What's Georama?

—If you don't know what a simple English word means, the Brothers in Synge Street can't be making much of a hand of you. A georama is a globe representing the earth. Something like what they have in schools. The sound of it goes well with general and gymnasium. That's why I took it. Join the GGG.

—And where did all those postal orders come from?

—From the other side. I put a small ad in one of the papers. I want to teach people to walk the high wire.

—Is that what the General Georama Gymnasium is for, for heaven's sake?

—Yes. And it's one of the cheapest courses in the world. A great number of people want to walk the high wire and show off. Some of them may be merely mercenary and anxious to make an easy, quick fortune with some great circus.

—And are you teaching them this by post?

—Well, yes.

—What's going to happen if one of them falls and gets killed?

—A verdict of death by misadventure, I suppose. But it's most unlikely because I don't think any of them will dare to get up on the wire any distance from the ground. If they're young their parents will stop them If they're old, rheumatism, nerves and decayed muscles will make it impossible.

—Do you mean you're going to have a correspondence course with those people?

—No. They get a copy of my four-page book of instructions. Price sixpence only. It's for nothing. A packet of fags and a box of matches would cost you nearly that, and no fag would give you the thrill of thinking about the high wire.

—This looks to me like a swindle.

—Rubbish. I'm only a bookseller. The valuable instructions and explanations are given by Professor Latimer Dodds. And he has included warnings of the danger as well.

—Who is Professor Latimer Dodds?

—A retired trapeze and high-wire artist.

—I never heard of him.

—Here, take a look at the course yourself. I'm posting off copies just now to my clients.

I took the crudely printed folder he handed me and put it in my pocket, saying that I would look over it later and make sure that Mr. Collopy didn't see it. I didn't want the brother to appraise my reactions to his handiwork, for already I had a desire to laugh. Downstairs, Mr. Collopy was out and Annie was in the bedroom colloguing with Mrs. Crotty. I lit the gas and there and then had a sort of free lesson on how to walk the high wire. The front page or cover read "THE HIGH WIRE—Nature Held at Bay—Spine-chilling Spectacle Splenetizes Sporting Spectators—By Professor H. Q. Latimer Dodds."

Lower down was the title of the Gymnasium and our own address. There was no mention of the brother by name but a note said "Consultations with the Director by appointment only." I was horrified to think of strangers calling and asking Mr. Collopy to be good enough to make an appointment for them with the Director of the Gymnasium.

The top of the left inside page had a Foreword which I think I may quote:

It were folly to asseverate that periastral peripatesis on the *aes ductile*, or wire, is destitute of profound peril not only to sundry *membra,* or limbs, but to the back and veriest life itself. Wherefore is the reader most graciously implored to abstain from *le risque majeur* by first submitting himself to the most perspicacious scrutiny by highly qualified physician or surgeon for, in addition to anatomical verifications, evidence of Ménière's Disease, caused by haemorrhage into the equilibristic labyrinth of the ears, causing serious nystagmus and insecurity of gait. If giddiness is suspected to derive from gastric disorder, resort should be had to bromide of potassium, acetanilide, bromural or chloral. The aural labyrinth consists of a number of membranous chambers and tubes immersed in fluid residing in the cavity of the inner ear, in mammals joined to the cochlea. The membranous section of the labyrinth consists of two small bags, the saccule and the utricle, and three semicircular canals which open into it. The nerves which supply the labyrinth end with a number of cells attired in hairlike projections which, when grouped, form the two otolith organs in the saccule and utricle and the three *cristae* of the semicircular canals. In the otolith organs the hairlike protuberances are embedded in a gelatinous mass containing calcium carbonate. The purpose of this grandiose apparatus, so far as *homo sapiens* is concerned, is the achievement of remaining in an upright posture, one most desirable in the case of a performer on the high wire who is aloft and far from the ground.

I found that conscientiously reading that sort of material required considerable concentration. I do not know what it means and I have no doubt whatever that the brother's "clients" did not know either.

The actual instructions as to wire-walking were straightforward enough. Perhaps it was the brother's own experience (for he was undoubtedly Professor Latimer Dodds) which made him advise a bedroom as the scene of opening practices. The wire was to be slung about a foot from the floor between two beds very heavily weighted "with bags of cement, stone, metal safes or other ponderous objects." When the neophyte wire-walker was ready to begin practice, the massive bedsteads were to be dragged apart by "friends," so that the necessary tension of the wire would be established and maintained. "If it happens that the weight on a bed turns out to be insufficient to support the weight of the performer on the wire, the friends should sit or lie on the bed." Afterwards practice was transferred to "the orchard" where two stout adjacent fruit trees were to be the anchors of the wire, the elevation of which was to be gradually increased. The necessity for daily practice was emphasized and (barring accidents) a good result was promised in three months. A certain dietetic regimen was pre

scribed, with total prohibition of alcohol and tobacco, and it was added that even if the student
proved absolutely hopeless in all attempts at wire-
walking, he would in any event feel immensely im-
proved in health and spirits at the end of that three
months.

I hastily put the treatise in my pocket as I heard
the steps of Mr. Collopy coming in the side door.
He hung his coat up on the back of the door and
sat down at the range.

—A man didn't call about the sewers? he asked.

—The sewers? I don't think so.

—Ah well, please God he'll be here tomorrow.
He's going to lay a new connection in the yard,
never mind why. He is a decent man by the name
of Corless, a great handball player in his day.
Where's that brother of yours?

—Upstairs.

—Upstairs, faith! What is he doing upstairs? Is
he in bed?

—No. I think he's writing.

—Writing? Well, well. Island of Saints and
Scholars. Upstairs writing and burning the gas. Tell
him to come down here if he wants to write.

Annie came out of the back room.

—Mrs. Crotty would like to see you, Father.

—Oh, certainly.

I went upstairs to warn the brother. He nodded
grimly and stuffed a great wad of stamped envelopes, ready for the post, under his coat. Then he
put out the gas.

7

ANY months had passed and the situation in our kitchen was as many a time before: myself and the brother were at the table weaving the web of scholarship while Mr. Collopy and Father Fahrt were resting themselves at the range with the crock, tumblers and a jug of water between them.

The plumber Corless had long ago come and

gone, ripping up the back yard and carrying out various mysterious works, not only there but in Mrs. Crotty's bedroom. Sundry lengths of timber had been delivered for Mr. Collopy himself and, since these things went on mostly while the brother and I were at school, we were told by Annie that the hammering and constructional bedlam to be heard from the sick woman's room were "very sore on the nerves." It was a point of apathy, or tact, or safety-first with the brother and myself to ask no questions as to what was afoot or evince any curiosity. "They might only be making a coffin," the brother said to me, "and of course that's a very religious business. People can be very sensitive there. We are better minding our own business."

On this evening Mr. Collopy had given an incoherent little cry.

—A pipe, Collopy. Just a pipe.

—And when did this start?

—It is a fortnight now.

—Well . . . I see no objection if it suits you, though I think it's a bad habit and a dirty habit. Creates starch in the stomach, I believe.

—Like many a thing, Father Fahrt said urbanely, it is harmless in moderation. Please God I will not become an addict . . .

Here he peremptorily scratched himself about the back.

—Haven't I one cross to bear as it is? But the doctor I saw recently thought my mind was a bit inclined to wander, a very bad thing in our Order.

Father Superior voiced the view that I was doing too much work, perhaps. I would not take a drug, so the doctor said tobacco in moderation was a valuable sedative. He smokes himself, of course. This pipe was a penance for the first week. But now it is good. Now I can think.

—I'll keep my eye on you and by dad I might follow suit myself, starch and all. I needn't tell you I also have my worries . . . my confusions. My work is inclined to get out of hand.

—You will win, Collopy, for your persistence is heroic. The man whose aim is to smooth out the path of the human race cannot easily fail.

—Well, I hope that's true. Give me your glass.

Here new drinks were decanted with sacramental piety and precision.

—It's a queer thing, Father Fahrt mused, that men in my position have again and again to attack the same problem, solve it, and yet find that the solution is never any easier to reach. Next week I have to give a retreat at Kinnegad. After that, other retreats at Kilbeggan and Tullamore.

—Hah! Kilbeggan? That's where my little crock here came from, refilled a hundred times since. And emptied a hundred times too, by gob.

—I like to settle on a central theme for a retreat. Often it is not simple to think of a good one. No hell-fire preaching by our men, of course.

Mr. Collopy nodded, reflectively. When eventually he spoke there was impatience in his voice.

—You Jesuits, Father, are always searching for

nice little out-of-the-way points, some theological
rigmarole. Most of you fellows think you are
Aquinas. For God's sake haven't you got the Ten
Commandments? What we call the Decalogue?

—Ah, Saint Thomas! Yes, in his *Summa* he has
many interesting things to say about the same
Decalogue. So had Duns Scotus and Nicolaus de
Lyra. Of course it is the true deposit.

—Mean to say, why don't the people of this country obey the Ten Commandments given in charge
of Moses? "Honour thy father and thy mother."
The young people of today think the daddy is a
tramp and the mammy a poor skivvy. Isn't that
right?

Here the brother coughed.

—Oh no, Father Fahrt said.

He also coughed here but I think the pipe was
responsible.

—It is just that young people are a bit thoughtless. I would say you were as bad as the rest, Collopy, when you were a young fellow.

—Yes, Father. I could trust you to say that. I suppose you also think I coveted my neighbour's wife?

—No, Collopy, not while you were a young fellow.

—*What?* You mean when I grew up to man's
estate——

—No, no, Collopy, it is my jest.

—Faith then and I don't think the Commandments are the right thing for God's anointed to be
funny about. I never put my hand near a married

woman and there are two of them on my committee, very valuable, earnest souls.

—What nonsense! I know that.

—You want to scarify the divils in the town of
Kinnegad? There are pubs in that place. What
about our other old friend "Thou shalt not steal"?

—A much neglected ordinance.

—Well, if the pishrogues of publicans there are
anything like the Dublin ones, they are hill-and-
dale robbers. They water the whiskey and then give
you short measure. They give you a beef sandwich
with no beef in it, only scraws hacked off last Sunday's roast by the mammy upstairs with her dirty
hands. Some of those people don't wash themselves for weeks on end and that's a fact. Do you
know why some of those ladies often miss Mass?
They'd have to wash themselves. And darn their
damned stockings.

—As usual I think you exaggerate, Collopy.

—And false witness, is it? There's people in this
town that can't open their jaws without spilling out
a flood of lies and slanders. To biting a nice ripe
apple they would prefer backbiting any day.

—Yes, the tongue can be reckless.

—And adultery? The Lord save us! Don't talk to
me about adultery.

—I know, Collopy, that you are devoted to
women and their wants. But I am afraid that they
are not *all* angels. Sometimes one meets the tempt-
ress. You mentioned biting a ripe apple. Do not
forget the Garden of Eden.

—Baah! Adam was a damn fool, a looderamawn if you like. Afraid of nobody, not even the Almighty. A sort of poor man's Lucifer. Why didn't he tell that strap of a wife he had to go to hell?

—Excuse me, Father Fahrt.

That heart of mine, faultless registrar, gave a little jump of dismay. It was the brother, again interrupting his betters. They turned and stared at him, Mr. Collopy frowning darkly.

—Yes, Manus?

—The wife of Adam in the Garden of Eden was Eve. She brought forth two sons, Cain and Abel. Cain killed Abel but afterwards in Eden he had a son named Henoch. Who was Cain's wife?

—Well, Father Fahrt said, there has been disputation on that point already.

—Even if Eve had a daughter not mentioned, she would be Cain's sister. If she hadn't, then Cain must have married his own mother. Either way it seems to be a bad case of incest.

—What sort of derogatory backchat is that you are giving out of you about the Holy Bible? Mr. Collopy bellowed.

—I'm only asking, the brother said doggedly.

—Well, may God in his mercy help us. The father and the mother of a good thrashing is what *you* badly need.

—Now, now, Father Fahrt said smoothly, that question has been examined by the Fathers. What we nowadays know by the term incest was not sinful in the case of our first parents, since it was in-

evitable if the human race was to survive. We will
discuss it another time, Manus, you and I.

—That's right, Father, Mr. Collopy said loudly.
Encourage him. Give your blessing to the badness
that's in him. By damn but I'll have a word with
Brother Cruppy in Westland Row. I'll tell him——

He broke off here and we all sat still. It came
again, a faint cry from Mrs. Crotty's room.

—Is *Father Fahrt there?*

Mr. Collopy got up and hurried in, closing the
door tight.

—Ah, please God there is nothing wrong, Father
Fahrt said softly.

We sat in silence, looking at each other. After
some minutes Mr. Collopy reappeared.

—She would like to see you, Father, he said in a
strange low voice.

—Of course, the priest said, rising.

He gently went into where I knew only a candle
served. Mr. Collopy slumped back into his chair,
preoccupied, quite unaware of ourselves at the
table. Mechanically he sipped his drink, staring at
the gleam of the fire through the bars of the range.
The brother nudged me and rolled his eyes.

—Ah dear O, Mr. Collopy murmured sadly.

He poured another drink into his glass, nor did
he forget Father Fahrt.

—We know not the day . . . nor the hour. All
things come to him who waits. It's the very divil.

Again he slumped into silence, and for what
seemed a long, long time there was no sound at all

except that of the alarm clock above the range, which we began to hear for the first time. In the end Father Fahrt came quietly from the room and sat down.

—I am very pleased, Collopy, he said.

Mr. Collopy looked at him anxiously.

—Was it, he asked, was it . . . ?

—She is at peace. Her little harmless account is clear. Here we see God's grace working. She is at peace. She was smiling when I left her. The poor thing is very ill.

—You . . . did the needful?

—Surely. A sweet, spiritual safeguard is not another name for death. Often it means a miraculous recovery. I know of many cases.

The brother spoke.

—Should I go for Dr. Blennerhassett?

—No, no, Mr. Collopy said. He is due to call tonight anyway.

—Let us not be presumptuous, Collopy, Father Fahrt said gently. We do not know God's ways. She may be on her feet again in two weeks. We should pray.

But in four days Mrs. Crotty was dead.

8

ABOUT the time of Mrs. Crotty's death, the brother's "business" had grown to a surprising size. He had got a box—fitly enough, a soap box—from Davies the grocer's, and went down to the hall every morning very early to collect the little avalanche of letters awaiting him there before they should come to the notice of Mr. Collopy. Still using our home address, he had become, in addition to Professor Latimer Dodds, The Excelsior Turf Bureau, operated, I suspect, on the old system of dividing clients into groups equal to the number of runners in a given race, and sending a different horse with any chance to each group. No matter which horse won, a group of clients would have backed it, and one of the brother's rules of business was that a winning client should send him the odds to five shillings. He was by now smoking openly in the house and several times I saw him coming out of or going into a public house, usually with a rather down-at-heel character. He had money to spend.

He also operated the Zenith School of Journalism, which claimed to be able to explain how to make a fortune with the pen in twelve "clear, analytical, precise and unparagoned lessons." As well he was trying to flood Britain with a treatise on cage birds, published by the Simplex Nature Press, which also issued a Guide to Gardening, both works obviously composed of material looted from books in the National Library. He had put away his little press and now had printing done by an impoverished back-lane man with some small semblance of machinery. He once asked me to get stamps for him, giving me two pounds: this gives some idea of the volume of his correspondence.

He seemed in a bad temper the evening the remains of Mrs. Crotty were brought to the church at Haddington Road; he did not come home afterwards but walked off without a word, possibly to visit a public house. Next morning dawned dark, forbidding and very wet, suitable enough, I thought, for a funeral. I thought of Wordsworth and his wretched "Pathetic Fallacy." The brother, still in a bad temper, went down as usual to collect his mail.

—To hell with this house and this existence, he said when he came back. Now we will have to trail out to Deansgrange in this dirty downpour.

—Mrs. Crotty wasn't the worst, I said. Surely you don't begrudge her a funeral? You'll need one yourself some day.

—She was all right, he conceded. It's her damned husband I'm getting very tired of . . .

Mr. Hanafin called with his cab for myself, the brother, Mr. Collopy and Annie. The hearse and two other cabs were waiting at the church, the cabs accommodating mysterious other mourners who hurried to Mr. Collopy and Annie with whispers and earnest handshakes. Myself and the brother were ignored. As the Mass was about to begin, a third cab arrived with three elderly ladies and a tall, emaciated gentleman in severe black. These, I gathered later, were members of the committee assisting Mr. Collopy in his work, whatever that was.

The hearse elected to take the route along Merrion Road by the sea, where a sort of hurricane was in progress. The cabs following stumbled on the exposed terrain. Mr. Collopy, showing some signs of genuine grief, spoke little.

—Poor Mrs. Crotty was very fond of the sea, he said at last.

—Seemingly she was, Annie remarked. She told me once that when she was a girl, nothing could keep her out of the sea at Clontarf. She could swim and all.

—Yes, a most versatile woman, Mr. Collopy said. And a saint.

A burial on a wet day, with the rain lashing down on the mourners, is a matter simply of squalor. The murmured Latin at the graveside seemed to make the weather worse. The brother, keeping well to the back of the assembly, was quietly cursing in an undertone. I was surprised and indeed a bit shocked to see him surreptitiously taking a flat half-pint bottle from his hip pocket and, with grimaces, swallowing deep draughts from it. Surely this was unseemly at the burial of the dead? I think Father Fahrt noticed it.

When all was over and the sodden turgid clay in on top of the deceased, we made for the gate. Mr. Collopy was walking with a breathless stout man who had come on foot. When it was made known to us that this poor man had no conveyance, the brother gallantly offered his seat in the cab; this was gratefully accepted. The brother said he could borrow a bicycle near by but I was certain his plan was to borrow more than a bicycle, for there was a pub at Kill Avenue, which was also near by.

On the way home Mr. Collopy was a bit more animated, no doubt relieved that a painful stage in the ordeal was over, and introduced us to the stranger as Mr. Rafferty.

—I will not say, Rafferty, he said, that what-you-know was the sole reason for the woman's demise. Not the *sole* reason, mind you. But by Christ it had plenty to do with it.

—Don't you know it had, Mr. Rafferty said. Can't you be bloody sure it had. Lord save us, you'd wonder is this a Christian country at all.

—It's a country of crawthumpers.

—I had an idea the other night, Mr. Collopy. In two years there will be a Corporation election. I believe you own your own house and you would be eligible for membership. Why not go forward as a candidate? You could put down a motion at the City Hall and shame all that bastards. The Town Clerk could be ordered to instruct the City Engineer or Surveyor or whatever he is called to dot the town with what we need.

—I thought of that, Mr. Collopy replied. But two years, you said? Only the Almighty knows how many unfortunate women would be brought to an early grave in that time. Ah, man alive, the worry and trouble of it all might even bring myself there.

—Now don't be letting silly thoughts like that come into your head. Ireland needs you and you know that.

Mr. Rafferty, politely refusing an invitation to come all the way with us, was dropped off at Ballsbridge. When we reached the house, we took off our dripping coats, Mr. Collopy poked up the fire in the range, quickly had the crock on view, and sank into his chair.

—Annie, he said, get me three glasses.

When these were produced, he poured three generous measures of whiskey into each and added a little water.

—On a morning like this, he said ceremoniously, and on a sad occasion like this, I think everyone here is entitled to a good stiff drink if we're not going to get our death of cold. I disapprove of anybody taking strong drink before the age of forty-five but in God's name let us take it as medicine. It is better than all those pills and drugs and falthalals those ruffians in the chemist shops will give you, first-class poison for the liver and kidneys.

We drank to that; for me it was my first taste of whiskey but I was surprised to find that Annie treated the occasion quite casually, as if she was used to liquor. I found it made me drowsy, and I decided to go to bed for a few hours. I did so and slept soundly. I got up about five and was not long back in the kitchen when the brother came in. Mr. Collopy had evidently spent the entire interval with the crock and did not notice the brother much or the unseemly fact that he was drunk. There is no other word for it: drunk. He sat down heavily and looked at Mr. Collopy.

—On a day like this, Mr. Collopy, he said, I think I might have a drop of that tonic you have there.

—For once I think you are right, Mr. Collopy replied, and if you will get another glass we will see what can be done.

The glass was got and generously furnished. I was offered nothing and the drinking went on in silence. Annie began to lay the table for tea.

—I don't think, Mr. Collopy said at last, that there will be any need for you boys to go to school tomorrow and maybe the day after. Mourning, you know. The Brothers will understand.

The brother put his glass down on the range with a clinking thud.

—Is that so, Mr. Collopy? he said in a testy voice. Well now, is that so? Let me tell you this. I am not going back to that damned school tomorrow, the day after or any day.

Mr. Collopy started up in astonishment.

—What was that? he asked.

—I've left school—from today. I've had my bellyful of the ignorant guff that is poured out by those maggots of Christian Brothers. They're illiterate farmers' sons. They probably got their learning at some dirty hedge school.

—Will you for pity's sake have some respect for the cloth of those saintly servants of God, Mr. Collopy said sharply.

—They're not servants of God, they are slaves to their own sadistic passions, they are humbugs and impostors and a disgrace to their cloth. They are ruining the young people of this country and taking pride in their abominable handiwork.

—Have you no shame?

—I have more shame than those buggers have. Anyhow, I'm finished with school for good. I want to earn my living.

—Well now, is that so? Doing what? Driving a tram or a breadcart, or maybe sweeping up after the horses on the roads?

—I said I wanted to earn my living. What am I talking about—I *am* earning my living. I am a publisher, an international tutor. Look at that!

Here he had rummaged in his inside pocket and pulled out a spectacular wad of notes.

—Look at that, he cried. There's about sixty-five pounds in that bundle and upstairs I have twenty-eight pounds in postal orders not yet cashed. You have your pension and no work to do, and no desire to do any.

—That will do you, Mr. Collopy retorted with rising temper, that is quite enough. You say I have no work to do. Where you got that information I cannot say. But let me tell you this, you and your brother. I have been engaged on one of the most ardious and patriotic projects ever attempted by any man in this town. You will hear all about it when I'm gone. You have a damned cheek to say I do no work. What, with my health in the state it's in?

—Don't ask me that. I've left school and that's all.

The subject seemed to become inert and was dropped. It had been a tiring day, physically and emotionally, and both Mr. Collopy and the brother were the worse for drink. Later, in bed, the brother asked me whether I intended to continue going to the Brothers in Synge Street.

—I might as well for the present, I replied, until I can find some job to fit into.

—Please yourself, he said, but I don't think this place is suitable for me. An Irish address is no damned use. The British dislike and distrust it. They think all the able and honest people live in London. I am giving that matter some thought.

9

URING the year that followed Mrs.
Crotty's death, the atmosphere of the house
changed somewhat. Annie joined some sort of a
little club, probably composed mostly of women
who met every afternoon to play cards or discuss
household matters. She seemed to be—heavens!—
coming out of her shell. Mr. Collopy returned to
his mysterious work with renewed determination,

not infrequently having meetings of his committee in our kitchen after warning everybody that this deliberative chamber was out of bounds for that evening. From an upper window I occasionally saw the arrival of his counsellors. Two elderly ladies and the tall, gaunt man of the funeral came, also Mr. Rafferty with a young lady who looked to me, in the distance at least, to be pretty.

The brother went from strength to strength and eventually reached the stage of prosperity that is marked by borrowing money for industrial expansion. From little bits of information and from inference, I understood that he had borrowed £400 short-term with interest at twenty per cent. A quick turnover, no matter how small the profit, was the brother's business axiom. He happened to read about the discovery in an old English manor house of 1,500 two-volume sets of a survey in translation of Miguel de Cervantes Saavedra, his work and times. The volumes were very elegant, bound in leather and handsomely illustrated; the first contained an account of the life of Cervantes, the second extracts from his major works. These volumes were printed and published in Paris in 1813, with a consignment apparently shipped to England, stored and forgotten. A London bookseller bought the lot for a small sum and to him the brother wrote offering 3s. 6d. cash per set for the whole consignment. At the time I thought the transaction foolhardy, for surely the London man could be presumed to have had a clear idea of the market. But once again the brother seemed to know what he was about. Using the name of the Simplex Nature Press, he put advertisements into English newspapers recklessly praising the work as to content and format, and also making the public an astonishingly generous offer, viz., any person buying Volume I for 6s. 6d. would also get Volume II for absolutely nothing. The offer, which was of limited duration, could not be repeated. No fewer than 2,500 acceptances reached him, quite a few from colleges, and he was many times later to adopt this system of enticement, offering something for nothing. The deal showed a clear profit of about £121. It also indirectly affected myself, for when wooden packing cases began to arrive full of those memorials of Cervantes, he politely suggested that I should take my bed and other gear to another room which was empty, as the original room was now his "office" as well as his bedroom. I had no objection to this move, and agreed. Unfortunately the first four packing cases arrived when both myself and the brother were out, and Mr. Collopy had to sign for them. I was the first to arrive home to find them piled in the kitchen. Mr. Collopy was frowning from his chair.

—In God's name, he said loudly, what is that bucko up to?

—I don't know. I think there are books in those cases.

—*Books?* Well now! What sort of books is he peddling? Are they dirty books?

—Oh, I don't think so. They might be Bibles.

—Faith and that would take me to the fair altogether. You heard what he said about the pious and
godly Christian Brothers some months ago. Now
by the jappers he is all for being a missionary to
the niggers in Black Africa or maybe the Injuns.
Well, there's no doubt about it, we rare up strange
characters in this country. I don't think he knows
anything about the Word of God. I'm not sure that
he knows even his prayers.

—My mention of the Bible was only a guess, I
protested.

Mr. Collopy had risen and was at the press in
search of his crock and glass. Fortified with them,
he sat down again.

—We'll see what's in them all in good time, he
announced sternly, and if those books are dirty
books, lascivious peregrinations on the fringes of
filthy indecency, cloacal spewings in the face of
Providence, with pictures of prostitutes in their
pelts, then out of this house they will go and their
owner along with them. You can tell him that if
you see him first. And I would get Father Fahrt to
exorcise all fiendish contaminations in this kitchen
and bless the whole establishment. Do you hear
me?

—Yes, I hear.

—Where is he now?

—I don't know. He is a very busy man. Perhaps
he is at confession.

—The what was that?

—He might be seeing the clergy on some abstruse theological point.

—Well, *I'll* abstruse *him* if he is up to any tricks, because this is a God-fearing house.

I sat down to attack my loathsome homework with the idea of being free at eight o'clock so that I could meet a few of the lads for a game of cards. Mr. Collopy sat down quietly sipping his whiskey and gazing at the glare of the fire.

It was about eleven when I got home that night, to find no trace of Mr. Collopy nor the piled boxes. Next morning I learnt that Mr. Collopy had gone to bed early and the brother, arriving home about ten, went out again to summon Mr. Hanafin to assist him in getting the boxes up to his office. No doubt the reward was a handsome tip, though a soiled glass in the sink suggested that further recompense from the crock had been sought by either Mr. Hanafin or the brother himself. I warned the latter, before I set off for school, of Mr. Collopy's dire suspicions about the books and the threats to fire him out of the house. Was Cervantes an immoral writer?

—No, the brother said grimly, but I won't be long here in any case. I think I know how to fix the oul divil. Have a look at these books.

They were thick octavo volumes of real beauty in an old-fashioned way, and there were many clear pictures of the woodcut kind. If only as an adorn-

ment to bookshelves, they were surely good value
for six and sixpence.

Later in the day the brother cunningly inscribed
a dedication to Mr. Collopy in each volume and
ceremoniously presented them in the kitchen.

—At first, he told me, he was mollified, then he
was delighted and said I had very true taste. Cervantes, he said, was the Aubrey de Vere of Spain.
His *Don Quixote* was an immortal masterpiece of
the classics, clearly inspired by Almighty God. He
told me not to fail to send a copy to Father Fahrt.
I had to laugh. There's a *pair* of humbugs in it.
Can you give me a hand to do some packing? I
have bought a load of brown paper.

I had to, of course.

It was a peculiarity of the brother never to stop in
his tracks or rest on his oars. In a matter of days he
was back at work in his private mine, the National
Library.

After some weeks he asked my opinion of three
manuscripts he had compiled for issue as small
books by the Simplex Nature Press. The first was
the "Odes and Epodes of Horace, Done into English Prose by Dr. Calvin Knottersley, D.Litt.
(Oxon.)"; the second was "Clinical Notes on Pott's
Fracture, by Ernest George Maude, M.D.,
F.R.C.S."; and the third was "Swimming and Div-
ing. A Manly and Noble Art, by Lew Paterson." It
was clear that these compositions were other people's work rehashed but I offered no comment other

than a warning of the folly of making Dr. Maude a
Fellow of the Royal College of Surgeons. A register
of such Fellows was in existence, and somebody was
bound to check.

—How do you know there isn't a Fellow named
Maude? the brother asked.

—So much the worse if there is, I answered.

But I noticed later that the doctor had lost that
honour.

10

I was a vile night as we sat in the kitchen, Mr. Collopy and I. He was slumped at the range in his battered armchair, reading the paper. I was at the table, indolently toying with school exercises, sometimes pausing to reflect on the possibilities of getting a job. I was really sick of the waste of time known as study, a futile messing about with things which did not concern me, and

I rather envied the brother's free, almost gay, life. I could sense his growing maturity and his determination to make money, a lot of it, as quickly as possible without undue worry as to the methods used. This night he was out, possibly conferring on some new deal in a public house. Annie was also out.

There was a knock and I admitted Father Fahrt. Mr. Collopy greeted him without rising.

—Evening, Father. And isn't it a caution!

—Ah yes, Collopy, but we had a good summer, thank God. You and I don't go out much, anyway.

—I think we deserve a smahan, Father, to keep the winter out of us.

As Father Fahrt produced his pipe, now a treasured solace, Mr. Collopy dragged himself up, went to the press and took down the crock, two glasses, and fetched a jug of water.

—Now, he said.

Drinks were poured and delicately savoured.

—I will tell you a funny one, Father, Mr. Collopy said. A damn funny one. I will give you a laugh. We had a committee meeting last Wednesday. Mrs. Flaherty was there. She told us all about her dear friend, Emmeline Pankhurst. Now there is a bold rossie for you if you like, but she's absolutely perfectly right. She'll yet do down that scoundrel Lloyd George. I admire her.

—She has courage, Father Fahrt agreed.

—But wait till you hear. When we got down to

our own business, discussing ways and means and ekcetera, out comes the bold Mrs. Flaherty with *her* plan. Put a bumb under the City Hall!

—Lord save us!

—Blow all that bastards up. Slaughter them. Blast them limb from limb. If they refuse to do their duty to the ratepayers and to humanity they do not deserve to live. If they were in ancient Rome they would be crucified.

—But Collopy, I thought you were averse to violence.

—That may be, Father, that may well be. But Mrs. Flaherty isn't. She would do all those crooked corporators in in double-quick time. What she calls for is *action*.

—Well, Collopy, I trust you explained the true attitude to her—your own attitude. Agitation, persistent exposure of the true facts, reprimand of the negligence of the Corporation, and the rousing of public opinion. Whatever Mrs. Flaherty could do on those lines, now that she is at large, there is little she could do if she were locked up in prison.

—She wouldn't be the first in this country, Father, who went to prison for an ideal. It's a habit with some people here.

—For public agitation you must be in the middle of the public. They must see you.

—How would the Church look on Mrs. Flaherty's scheme?

—I have no doubt it would merit strong condemnation and censure. Such a thing would be highly sinful. I think it could be classed as murder. It is not lawful to kill to ameliorate public misrule or negligence. Assassination is never justified. One must put one's trust in elections and the vote, not in shedding human blood.

—I fear, Father Fahrt, that that is the gospel of chicks and goslings. My forebears were brave, strong-arm fellows. And what about the early Christian martyrs? They thought nothing of shedding their own blood in defence of a principle. Give me your glass.

—There is no comparison, of course. Thanks.

—Now listen here, Father. Listen carefully. This is the first part of November. In the year 1605 in England, King James the First was persecuting the Catholics, throwing them into prison and plundering their property. It was diabolical, worse than in Elizabeth's time. The R.C.s were treated like dogs, and their priests like pigs. It would put you in mind of the Roman emperors, except that a thullabawn like Nero could at least boast that he was providing public entertainment. Well, what happened?

—James was a very despicable monarch, Father Fahrt said slowly.

—I will tell you what happened. A man named Robert Catesby thinks to himself that we've had as much of this sort of carry-on as we're going to take. And he thought of the same plan as Mrs. Flaherty. He planned to blow up the parliament house and annihilate the whole bloody lot of the bosthoons, his Majesty included. I know the thanks you'd get if you told *him* to busy himself with elections and votes. He'd slap your face and give you a knee in the belly. Remember, remember the Fifth of November.

—They lived in another age, of course, Father Fahrt answered.

—Right and wrong don't change with the times and you know that very well, Father. Catesby got Guy Fawkes on his side, a brave man that was fighting in Flanders. And Grant and Keyes and the two Winters, any God's amount of sound men, Romans all. Fawkes was the kingpin and the head bottlewasher of the whole outfit. He managed to get a ton and a half of gunpowder stuffed into a cellar under the House of Lords. But there were two other men lending a good hand all the time and saying God bless the work. I mean Greenway and Garnet. Know who *they* were, Father?

—I think I do.

—Of course you do. They were *Jesuits.* Hah?

—My dear man, Jesuits also can make mistakes. They can err in judgement. They are human.

—Faith then they didn't err in judgement when Guy Fawkes was found out. They scooted like greased lightning and Father Greenway and another priest managed to get to a healthier country. Father Garnet was not so alive to himself. He got caught and for his pains he got a length of hempen rope for himself, on the gallows high.

—A martyr for the Faith, of course, Father Fahrt said evenly.

—And Fawkes. They gave him tortures you wouldn't see outside hell itself to make him give the names of the others. Be damn but he wouldn't. But when he heard that Catesby and a crowd of his segocias had been chased, caught and killed, he broke down and made some class of a confession. But do you know what? When this rigmarole was put before him for signature, believe it or not but he couldn't sign it. The torture had him banjaxed altogether. His hands were all broken be the thumb-screws. What's your opinion of that?

—The torture Fawkes so heroically endured, Father Fahrt said, was admittedly appalling and ter-rifying, the worst torture that the head of man could think of. It was called *per gradus ad ima*. He was subjected to it by direct order of the King. He was very brave.

—I needn't tell you he and several others got the high jump. But Lord save us, poor Fawkes couldn't climb up the ladder to the gallows, he was so badly bet and broken up in the torture. He had to be car-ried up. And he was hanged outside the building he tried to blow up for the greater glory of God.

—I suppose that's true enough, Father Fahrt said meekly.

—For the greater glory of God. How's this you put Latin on that?

—*Ad majorem Dei gloriam.* It is our own So-ciety's watchword.

—Quite right. A.M.D.G. Many a time I've heard it. But if blowing up councillors is bad and sinful as you said, how do you account for two Jesuits, maybe three, being guilty of that particular transaction, waging war on the civil power? Isn't Mrs. Flaherty in the same boat as Mr. Fawkes?

—I have pointed out, Collopy, that events and opinions vary drastically from one era to another. People are influenced by quite different things in dissimilar ages. It is difficult, even impossible, for the people of today to assess the stresses and atmosphere of Fawkes's day. Cicero was a wise and honest man and yet he kept slaves. The Greeks were the most sophisticated and civilized people of antiquity, but morally a great many of them were lepers. With them sins of the flesh was a nefarious preoccupation. But that does not invalidate the wisdom and beauty of the things many of them left behind them. Art, poetry, literature, architecture, philosophy and political systems, these were formulated and developed in the midst of debauchery. I have —ah-ha—sometimes thought that a degraded social climate is essential to inspire great men to achievement in the arts.

Mr. Collopy put down his glass and spoke somewhat sternly, wagging a finger.

—Now look at here, Father Fahrt, he said, I'm going to say something I've said in other ways before. Bedamn but I don't know that I can trust you men at all. Ye are forever trimming and adjudicating yourselves to the new winds that do blow. In case of doubt, send for a Jesuit. For your one doubt he will give you twenty new ones and his talk is always full of "ifs" and "buts," rawmaish and pseudo-theology. The word I have heard used for that sort of thing is *casuistry*. Isn't that right? Casuistry.

—There is such a word but it's not true in this case.

—Oh now, you can always trust a Jesuit to make mischief and complicate simple things.

—That word Jesuit. Our founder Ignatius was a Spaniard and had a different name for the Order, but it was called Societas Jesu by command of the Holy Father Paul III. Originally the title Jesuit was one of hatred and contempt. What was intended as an insult we accepted as a compliment.

—I suppose that's what I mean—you are for ever double-thinking and double-talking. You slither everywhere like quicksilver. There's no pinning a Jesuit down. Then we're told it is a mendicant order. Sure there isn't a better-got collection of men on the face of the earth, churches and palaces all over the world. I know a thing or two. I've read books. I'll tell you something about 35 Lower Leeson Street, the poor cave you hide in yourself.

—What?

—The emaciated friars in that place have red wine with their dinners. That's more than Saint Peter himself had. But Saint Peter got himself into a sort of divarsion with a cock. The holy Fathers below in Clongowes Wood know all about cocks, too. They have them roasted and they eat them at dinner. And they are great men for scoffing claret.

—Such talk is most unworthy. We eat and drink according to our means. The suggestion that we are, well . . . sybarites and gluttons is nonsense. And offensive nonsense, Collopy. I do not like such talk.

—Well is that so? Mr. Collopy said testily. Is criticizing the Jesuits a new sin? Would you give somebody five rosaries in the confessional for that? Faith then, if criticizing the Jesuits is a fall from grace, let us say a Hail Mary for the repose of the soul of Pope Paul IV, for he told Ignatius Loyola there were a lot of things wrong with the Order that would have to be put right. Did you know that? And did Ignatius bend the knee in front of the Holy Father? Not on your life. Give me your damn glass.

—Thanks. I do not say that Ignatius was without fault. Neither was Peter. But Ignatius was canonized in 1622 by Pope Gregory XV, only sixty-six years after his death. He is now in Paradise.

—You know he died without the last rites?

—I do. He was called suddenly. He was weak of body but his labours in this world were prodigious, and nobody can take from him credit for the great deed of founding the Order, which is now and ever has been the intellectual vanguard of the Catholic Church.

—I wouldn't say the story is quite so simple as that, Father Fahrt. By dad, the same Order caused a lot of bad bloody ructions at one time.

—The Fathers are all over the world, they speak

and write in all languages, they have built a wonderful apparatus for the propagation of the faith.

—Some people at one time thought they were trying to banjax and bewilder the One, Holy and Apostolic. Oh and there are good people who are alive today and think the Church had a very narrow escape from the boyos of yesteryear.

—I know it is useless asking who those important people are.

—In the days of my youth I met a Jesuit in Belfast and he said the Jesuits were the cause of the Franco-Prussian War and the Boer War, for ever meddling in politics, and keeping a sharp eye out for Number One—money.

—Do you tell me so? A Jesuit?

—Yes, a Jesuit. He was a married man, of course.

—Some dreadful apostate, you mean?

—He was a most religious man, and told me he hoped his daughter would become a nun.

—You must have been talking to the ghost of Martin Luther.

—I think the Jesuits are jealous of Luther. He also tried to destroy the Catholic Church. I often think he made a better attempt than you people did.

—Dear me, Collopy, you are very irresponsible. If you talked like that among strangers, you would be in grave danger of giving scandal, of leading others on to sin. You should be more circumspect.

—I am as fond of my altar and my home, Father Fahrt, as the next. But I revere truth. I *love* truth.

—Well, that is good news.

—I think you are fond of truth, too, provided it is the truth you like, the truth that suits your book.

—Nonsense. Truth is truth.

—There is a phrase in Irish—I'm sorry that through no fault of mine I am largely unacquainted with the old tongue. But the phrase says this: "The truth does be bitter." I think you know how right that is.

—*Magna est veritas et prevalebit.*

—You never said a truer word, Father.

—Aren't we the stupid and presumptuous pair to be talking in this loose way about the Order of men such as Ignatius and Francis Xavier?

—Hold on a moment now.

—Xavier was the evangelist of Japan. Jesuit evangelists preached the Gospel, often in face of persecution and martyrdom, to the Indians of North America, to the natives of the Philippines and the countries of South America, even to the English when the Catholic Church was proscribed there. They went everywhere. Nothing stopped them.

—Hold on a moment now, Father. Whisht now for a minute and listen to me. It is true that the Jesuits were everywhere and had a finger in every pie. They were cute hawks. They were far too powerful, not only in the Church itself but in the world. They made all sorts of kings and queens and captains take to themselves a Jesuit chaplain. Can you imagine Parnell with a Jesuit chaplain?

—Parnell was not a Catholic, and I don't believe

he was a real Irishman. Parnell is an English name.

—Those devout priests infested the courts of Europe and had the same courts in their pockets. They were sacerdotal politicians and that's what they were. Those ignorant and drunken princes and emperors were no match for them. Sure they'd excommunicate you as soon as they'd look at you.

—Nonsense. A priest has no power of excommunication.

—Maybe so. But hadn't they the bishop in their pockets as well? The bishop had to do as they ordered him.

—You're annoying me, Collopy. Here, play with this glass.

—Certainly. But there were two very great men in France, Pascal and Voltaire. That pair had no time for the Jesuits at all, and neither had the Jansenist crowd. Am I right?

—Yes, reasonably so.

—The Jesuits had rows with the Sorbonne, with the Franciscans and the Dominicans on questions of doctrine. A lot of pious and intelligent men thought the Jesuits were heretics or schismatics. Faith now and there was no smoke without fire— hell-fire, maybe. Onwards from 1760 or so, they were given their marching orders in Portugal, France and parts of Italy itself. Messengers and runners and wren-boys were dispatched wholesale by several states in Europe to Rome to try to bully the Pope into suppressing the Order. And fair enough, they weren't wasting their time. The Pope of that fine day was Clement XIV. Lo and behold, in 1773 he issued a Bull suppressing the Order because it could no longer carry out the work for which it was founded.

—Yes, Father Fahrt said, *Dominus ac Redemptor Noster.*

—Excuse me, I said.

It was brazenly cheeky on my part to try to emulate the brother as interlocutor. But my labours at school on Schuster's Church History were not to be denied.

—Yes? Mr. Collopy said rather grumpily.

—*Dominus ac Redemptor Noster* was not a Bull. It was a Brief. There is a difference.

—The boy is perfectly right, Father Fahrt said.

Mr. Collopy did not like the pedantic intrusion.

—Call the thing what you like, he said crankily, the fact remains that the Holy Father suppressed the Society. That was a matter of faith and morals and in doing that the Pope was infallible.

—Collopy, Father Fahrt said sharply, that merely proves again that you do not know what you are talking about. It was not till 1870, when Pius IX was pontiff, that the Vatican Council proclaimed the dogma of papal infallibility. You are almost one hundred years out. Furthermore, the suppression of a religious order has nothing to do with faith and morals in the universal church.

—You are being technical as usual, Father, Mr. Collopy said in a bantering tone. Hand over your glass like a good man.

—Thanks. Not much now.

—One of the bitterest objections to the machinations of the Jesuits was this. Some of the priests mixed up their missionary work with trading and money-making and speculation. A French Jesuit named Father La Valette was up to his ears in buying and selling. Mendicant order my foot.

—These were isolated cases.

—They were not. The Order was some class of an East India Company. It was heavenly imperialism but with plenty of money in the bank.

—Well, well. Speaking for myself, I have nothing at all in the bank but I have my tramfare in my pocket, thank God.

—And where do you get that tobacco you are smoking?

—From the Society's vast plantations in Panama. Father Fahrt said heavily. That suppression was a very serious blow and was the result of secret scheming by our agnostic enemies. Our missions in India, China and throughout Latin America collapsed. It was a victory for the Jansenists. It was a very sad episode.

—Fair enough, Mr. Collopy replied, but th'oul Jesuits weren't bet yet. Trust them! They soon started their counter-scheming. Oh trust Wily Willie, S.J.!

—It was their duty before God to try to salvage the Order. In Belgium some ex-Jesuits formed a new society named the "Fathers of the Faith." Catherine of Russia would not allow that Brief to take effect, and the Jesuits tried to carry on in that country. After a time the two communities merged. You can take it, Collopy, that my Order was on the way back from then.

—By damn but you are not telling me anything I don't know, Mr. Collopy said warmly. You couldn't keep that crowd down. Too cute.

—Is that what you think? Very good. This is a fresh drink. I am going to drink to the health, spiritual and physical, of my Society.

—I'll drink with you, Mr. Collopy said, but with mental reservations.

They had the toast between them in a preoccupied way.

—And let us devoutly remember, Father Fahrt said after a long pause, the great Bull *Sollicitudo Omnium Ecclesiarum*, promulgated on August the seventh, 1814, by Pope Pius VII after he returned from France. You know what that meant, Collopy?

—Well, I suppose your crowd got your way as usual.

—That Bull restored the Society throughout the whole world. And we were welcomed back in those countries which before had driven us out. Ah, the ways of the Almighty are surely a mystery.

—So are the ways of the Jesuits, Mr. Collopy said. Did any money change hands? Or was he one of the Popes who made a fortune selling scapulars and indulgences?

—Collopy, I think I have misjudged you. You are not serious. You are merely trying to annoy me.

You don't believe in what you say at all. As they say in Ireland, you are only trying to grig me. You ought to be ashamed of yourself. At the back of it all, you are a pious God-fearing man, may the Lord be good to you.

—I never make jokes about religious matters, Mr. Collopy said solemnly. If you want to praise me or compliment me, just give a thought to the important work I have been devoting my life to. The work that will not stop until this old heart stops.

—Well, what we have been discussing is a sort of a headline for you. Cherish in your heart a recollection of the tenacity of the Jesuit Fathers. If your aim is praiseworthy, you will achieve it by undeviating faith in it and by never ceasing to invoke the blessing of God on it. Don't you agree?

—What else have I been doing for years? By the jappers, it's a slow achievement I'm making of it. The divil himself is in the hearts of that Corporation ownshucks.

—They are just thoughtless, misguided.

—They are just a gang of ignorant, pot-bellied, sacrilegious, money-scooping robbers, very likely runners from the bogs, hop-off-my-thumbs from God-forsaken places like Carlow or the County Leitrim. The sons of pig-dealers and tinkers. In heaven's name what would people the like of that know about the duties of a city councillor? I wouldn't say they had a boot on their foot till they were eighteen.

—But shouldn't their clerks advise them? Surely *they're* Dublin men?

—That gurriers wouldn't think of advising a man to take off his clothes before he took a bath. Are you fooling me, Father?

—Indeed and I'm not.

Heavy steps were heard on the gravel outside and the handle of the door was turned.

It was the brother. One glance was enough for me. His face was flushed and he lurched slightly. In his hand was a small cigar, a bit the worse for the heavy rain outside.

—Good evening all, he said pleasantly enough. Good evening, Father Fahrt.

He sat down in the centre and spread his wet legs towards the range.

—I see we have got to cigars, Mr. Collopy said.

His mood was genial enough, thanks to the crock and his swordplay with Father Fahrt.

—Yes, we *have* got to cigars, the brother replied jauntily, just as Father Fahrt has progressed to the pipe. Degeneracy is contagious.

—And what important mission were we on to-night? Mr. Collopy asked.

—Well, since you ask me, it *was* important. Important for this house, and indeed this city, too. I have very bad news for you, Mr. Collopy. For all, in fact. This day week——

—What rodomondario is this you are giving us?

—This day week, I am leaving you. I am going to London to make my fortune.

—Well now! Is that a fact? Well the dear knows.

—London, my lad? Father Fahrt said. Well, well. It's a great place and there is opportunity there, but the English look for hard work. From the Irish, anyhow. I must give you a letter to some of our men over there. You have heard of Farm Street? But sometimes work is not so easy to get. You are not thinking of the coal-mining, are you?

Here the brother laughed, as if in genuine amusement.

—No, Father, he said, unless you mean buying a mine and putting enormous royalties into the bank.

—Well, what are you going to do? Mr. Collopy asked sharply.

—Well, what I've done so far is to take the lease of two rooms or offices in Tooley Street.

—And in God's name where is that?

—It is fairly central and very near the Thames. And there are several railway stations within easy distance. I mean, suppose the police were after me?

—The what? *The police?*

Mr. Collopy was not sure he had heard aright. The brother laughed again.

—Yes, the police. They'd hardly think of watching *all* the stations. Even if they did, there is a very good chance that I could escape by water. After I get settled down, I will have my private barge moored in the river. They will never suspect a move like that. We important men must think of everything.

—I think you are going off your head and it's not

the first time I thought that. What about money
for your passage and your lodgings beyond? If you
expect me——

—Mr. Collopy, you mustn't embarrass me with
such talk.

—So far as I remember, Father Fahrt interposed,
our people still run a shelter. Lay brothers are in
charge and I believe the cost per night is next to
nothing. I could give you a letter, of course.

—Have you got money? Mr. Collopy demanded.

—I have, or I will have during the week.

—Is it honest money? If there is any damned
nonsense about swindling anybody or robbing shops
or besting unfortunate simple people, I can tell you
plump and plain that you will not have to go as far
as London to make contact with the police. I would
not think twice of calling them in myself, for if
there is one thing that is abominable it is dis-
honesty. It is one of the worst inventions of Satan.
I don't want any curse brought on this house. You
have heard of Mayor Lynch of Galway? Mark that.
Mark that well.

—You are uncharitable, Collopy, Father Fahrt
said. Why assume bad things? Why meet the devil
halfway?

—I live in this house, Mr. Collopy said irritably,
and I have experience.

—For all we know, this enterprising young man
may yet bring great honour to this house.

—Yes indeed.

Mr. Collopy's tone had taken on a bitter edge.

—I myself may also bring great honour to this house by achieving the great aim of my life. Then they'll put a plaque on the wall outside and you will have women from all over the world coming on pilgrimages to see my humble house. By that time, of course, I'll be above in Deansgrange having a good rest for myself.

The brother yawned artificially.

—Gentlemen, he said, I'm tired and I want to get a night's sleep. We can talk more about my plans tomorrow.

He rose and stumbled out towards the stairs. We who remained looked at each other, mutely.

11

When I got to bed later the brother was asleep, no doubt in the anaesthesia of whiskey. In the morning I asked him whether he was serious about the project in Tooley Street.

—Course I'm serious, he answered.

—And what are you going to do there?

—I am going to open the London University Academy. I'll teach *everything* by correspondence, solve all problems, answer all questions. I might start a magazine first, and then a newspaper, but first I'll have to build up slowly. I'll teach the British how to learn French or cure chilblains. I'll be a limited company, of course. Already I have a solicitor working on the papers. My branch office will be the British Museum. If you like, I'll give you a job later on.

I suppose that was generous but for some reason the offer did not immediately attract me. Dryly I said:

—I'd want to get to know those railway stations you mentioned last night in case I had to skip. In a hurry.

—Don't talk rubbish. My operations are always within the law. But the British won't be nervous because if the bobbies were after me and managed to close the roads and railways and the river, haven't they the Tower of London to stuff me into? It's just across the river from Tooley Street.

—Well, many a good Irishman spent a time there.

—True.

—And lost his life.

—Well, I'll prepare and circulate a series entitled How to Escape from the Tower of London. Three guineas for the complete course, with daggers, revolvers and rope ladders supplied to students at very little over cost.

—Aw, shut up, I said.

When I got back from Synge Street that eve-

ning, everybody was out, but a note from Annie
said that my dinner was in the oven. Immediately
afterwards I attacked my damned homework, for I
had planned to spend the evening at a small poker
school in the home of my school friend Jack Mulloy. Did card games attract me much? I don't know,
but Jack's sister Penelope, who served mugs of tea
and bits of cake at "half-time," certainly did. She
was what was known as a good hoult, with auburn
hair, blue eyes and a very nice smile. And to be
honest, I think she was fond of myself. I remember
being puzzled to think that she and Annie belonged
to the same sex. Annie was a horrible, limp, lank
streel of a creature. But she had a good heart and
worked hard. Mr. Collopy was fussy about his meals
and though he dressed rather like an upper-class
tramp, he had a horror of laundries and mass washing. To participate in that, he held, was a certain
way to get syphilis and painful skin diseases. Annie
had to wash his shirts and other things, though he
personally looked after his celluloid collar, which
he washed with hot water every second day. She
also had to compound various medicines for him,
all of which contained sulphur, though I never
heard what afflictions those potions were intended
to remedy or prevent. In the last eighteen months
or so, she was asked to undertake another duty to
which she agreed willingly enough. The brother had
given up the early rising of his school days but
would often hand Annie some money for "what-
you-know" from his bedside. He was in need of a

cure, and the poor girl would slip out and bring him back a glass of whiskey.

Mr. Collopy came in about five o'clock, followed shortly afterwards by Annie. He seemed in a bad temper. Without a word he collapsed into his arm-chair and began reading the paper. The brother came in about six, loaded with books and small parcels. He naturally perceived the chill and said nothing. The tea turned out to be a very silent, almost menacing, meal. I kept thinking of Penelope. Tea with *her* would be a very different affair, an ambrosial banquet of unheard-of delicacy, and afterwards sweet colloquy by the fire, though perhaps with an undertone of melancholy. Was it easy, I wondered, or was it quite impossible to write really good and touching poetry? Something to reach the heart, to tell of love? Very likely it was quite impossible for the like of myself to attempt anything of the kind, though the brother could be trusted to explain the art and simplify it in six easy lessons by correspondence. Of course I never raised the matter with him, for he would only make me angry. Penelope? I meditated on the name. I remembered that Penelope was the wife of Ulysses and no matter how many libertines assailed her while her good man was away at the wars, she was ever faithful to him. She would consider yielding to their low and improper solicitations, she said, as soon as she had her knitting finished. Every night she would unravel whatever bit of it she had done during the day, so that the task was never accom-

plished. Just what was that as an attitude? Deep
and pure love, of course. With more than a little
touch of cunning, perhaps. Did my own lovely
Penelope have both those qualities? Well, I would
see her later on that night.

When the tea things had been cleared away,
Mr. Collopy resumed reading his paper, but after
a time he suddenly sat up and glared at the brother,
who was dozing opposite him at the range.

—I want a word with you, mister-me-friend, he
said abruptly.

The brother sat up.

—Well? he said. I'm here.

—Do you know a certain party by the name of
Sergeant Driscoll of the D.M.P.?

—I don't know any policemen. I keep far away
from them. They're a dangerous gang, promoted
at a speed that is proportionate to the number of
people they manage to get into trouble. And they
have one way of getting the most respectable people
into very bad trouble.

—Well is that a fact? And what is the one way?

—Perjury. They'd swear a hole in an iron bucket.
They are all the sons of gobhawks from down the
country.

—I mentioned Sergeant Driscoll of the
D.M.P.——

—The wilds of Kerry, I'll go bail. The banatee
up at six in the morning to get ready thirteen break-
fasts out of a load of spuds, maybe a few leaves of
kale, injun meal, salt and buttermilk. Breakfast for

Herself, Himself, the eight babbies and the three pigs, all out of the one pot. That's the sort of cods we have looking after law and order in Dublin.

—I mentioned Sergeant Driscoll of the D.M.P. He was here this morning. God help me, being interviewed by the police has been *my* cross, and at my time of life.

—Well, it is a good rule never to make any statement. Don't give him the satisfaction. Say that you first must see your solicitor, no matter what he is accusing you of.

—Accusing *me* of? It had nothing to do with me. It was *you* he was looking for. He was making inquiries. There may yet be deleterious ructions, you can take my word for that.

—What, *me*? And what have *I* done?

—A young lad fell into the river at Islandbridge, hurt his head and was nearly drowned. He had to be brought to hospital. Sergeant Driscoll and his men questioned this lad and the other young hooligan with him. And *your* name was mentioned.

—I know nothing about any young lads at Island-bridge.

—Then how did they get your name? They even knew this address, and the Sergeant said they had a little book with this address here on the cover.

—Did you see the book?

—No.

—This is the work of some pultogue that doesn't like me, one that has it in for me over some imaginary grievance. A trouble-maker. This town is full

of them. I'm damn glad I'm clearing out. Give me
a bloodthirsty and depraved Saxon any day.

—I've never known you not to have an answer.
You are the right stainless man.

—I refuse to be worried about what brats from
the slums say or think, or fat country rozzers either.

—Those youngsters, Sergeant Driscoll said, were
experimenting with a frightfully dangerous contrap-
tion, a sort of death machine. They had fixed a
wire across the Liffey, made fast to lampposts or
trees on either side. And this young bosthoon gets
his feet into a pair of special slippers or something
of the kind. What do you think of that?

—Nothing much, except it reminds me of a circus.

—Yes, or The Dance of Death at the Empire
Theatre at Christmas. Lord look down on us but I
never heard of such recklessness and sinful extrava-
ganza. It is the parents I pity, the suffering parents
that brought them up by wearing their fingers to
the bone and going without nourishing food in their
old age to give the young poguemahones an education. A touch of the strap, night and morning, is
what those boyos badly need.

—And how did one of them get into the water?

—How do you think? He gets out walking on
this wire until he's halfway, then he flies into a
panic, gets dizzy, falls down into the deep water,
hitting his head off a floating baulk of timber. And
of course not one of those thooleramawns could
swim. It was the mercy of God that a bailiff was

within earshot. He heard the screaming and the commotion and hurried up. But an unemployed man was there first. Between the pair of them they got this half-drowned young character out of the river and held him upside down to drain the water out of him.

—And the pinkeens, the brother interposed.

—It was a direct act of Providence that those men were there. The high-wire genius had to be lurried into hospital, Jervis Street, and there is no need to try to be funny about it. You could be facing murther today, or manslaughter.

—I've told you I had nothing to do with it. I know nothing. I am unaware of the facts.

—I suppose you'd swear that.

—I would.

—And you have the brazen cheek to sit there and accuse the long-suffering D.M.P. of being addicted to perjury.

—And so they are.

—Faith then, and if I was on the jury I would know who to believe about that Islandbridge affair.

—If I was charged with engineering that foolish prank, I would stop at nothing to unmask the low miscreant who has been trying to put stains on my character.

—Yes, I know right well what you mean. One lie would lead to another till you got so bogged down in mendacity and appalling perjury that the Master of the Rolls or the Recorder or whoever it would be would call a halt to the proceedings and send the papers to the Attorney-General. And faith then your fat would be in the fire. You could get five years for perjury and trying to pervert the course of justice. And the same Islandbridge case would be waiting for you when you came out.

—I don't give a goddam about any of those people.

—Do you tell me? Well, *I* do. This is my house.

—You know I'm leaving it very soon.

—And Sergeant Driscoll said you were to call at College Street for an interview.

—I'll call at no College Street. Sergeant Driscoll can go to hell.

—Stop using bad, depraved language in this house or you may leave it sooner than you think. You are very much mistaken if you think I am content to be hounded and pestered by policemen over your low and contemptible schemes to delude simple young people——

—Oh, rubbish!

—And rob them, rob them of money they never earned but filched from the purses of their long-suffering parents and guardians.

—I told you I don't know any simple young people at Islandbridge. And any young people I do know, they're not simple.

—You have one of the lowest and most lying tongues in all Ireland and that's a sure fact. You are nothing but a despicable young tramp. May God forgive me if I have been in any way to blame for the way I brought you up.

—Why don't you blame those crows, the holy Christian Brothers? God's Disjointed.

—I have warned you several times to stop desecrating my kitchen with your cowardly blackguarding of a dedicated band of high-minded Christian teachers.

—I hear Brother Cruppy is going to throw off the collar and get married.

— Upon my word, Mr. Collopy said shrilly, you are not too old to have a stick taken to. Remember that. A good thrashing would work wonders.

He was clearly very angry. The brother shrugged and said nothing but it was lucky just then that there was a knock at the outer door. It was Mr. Rafferty, who at first demurred at my invitation to come in.

—I was only passing, he said. I just wanted to see Mr. Collopy for a moment or two.

But he did come in. I was happy to see that the hostilities within had suddenly subsided. Mr. Collopy offered his hand without rising.

—Take a chair, Rafferty, take a chair. It's a bit hash this evening.

—Yes indeed, Mr. Collopy. Very hash.

—Will you join me in a smahan?

—Now, Mr. Collopy, you should know me by now. Weekends only. It's a rule and a cast-iron one. I promised the missus.

—All right, keep the promise. To thine old self

be true. Thine own self, I mean. I'll treat myself in
God's name because I am not feeling too good in
my health. Not too good at all.

He rose to go to the press.

—You know what I called for, of course?

—Indeed and I do. And I have it here.

Having arranged a glass with the crock on the
range, he pulled from the back of the press a long
brown paper parcel, which he laid carefully on the
table. Then he poured out his drink and sat down.

—The name they have for it, Rafferty, is worth
remembering.

He turned to my surprise to myself.

—You there, he said. What's the Greek for
water?

—*Hydor*, I said. High door.

—And measuring anything, how did the Greeks
get at that?

—*Metron*. Met her on. A measure.

—There now, Rafferty, didn't I tell you, what?
That article on the table is a clinical hydrometer.
As we agreed, you are to bring it to Mrs. Flaherty.
Tell her to take careful readings day and night for
a fortnight from next Saturday at noon. And keep
the most meticulous records.

—Oh, I understand how important that is, Mr.
Collopy. And I'll make Mrs. Flaherty understand.

—In these modern times, you are damn nothing
unless you can produce statistics. Columns and columns of figures, readings and percentages. Suppose
they set up a Royal Commission on this thing.

Where would we be if we couldn't produce our certified statistics? What would we look like in the witness chair?

—We would not be very impressive and that's a sure thing, Rafferty said.

—We'd look like bloody gawms. We'd make a holy show of ourselves before the world and people would ask each other who let us out. Isn't that right?

—Too right indeed.

—And when Mrs. Flaherty has given us her readings, we will give the next fortnight to Mrs. Clohessy.

—Very good idea, Mr. Collopy.

—And I predict one thing. When we have got all the readings and compared them, bedamn but you'll find very little difference in them, only slight variations. We might establish a great new scientific fact. Who knows?

—Do you tell me that, Mr. Collopy?

—I do, and that is the way the history of the whole world has been changed in the past. Patient men are looking for a particular thing, the answer to a profound difficulty. And what by the jappers happens? By accident they solve an entirely different problem. And I don't care how many problems are solved with the aid of the clinical hydrometer so long as what we ourselves are so worried about is put right.

—Hear, hear, Mr. Collopy. I'll go off now, and straight to Mrs. Flaherty's.

—And God be with you, Rafferty. See you at our usual committee on Friday night.

—Right. Good night.

Just after he left, I went out myself. For I had a tryst with the Sors—and with Penelope.

12

THE old kitchen seemed the same but the brother had gone, and with him those stormy little scenes with Mr. Collopy. I am sorry I cannot present an interesting record of the events and words of his actual departure. He had stressed with Annie the great importance of an early knock so as to make sure he would catch the morning mail boat from Kingstown to Holyhead. Annie did her duty

but she found nobody in the brother's bed nor any
sign of his packed belongings. He had stolen away
sometime in the night, perhaps finishing his last
Irish sleep in somebody else's house or, perhaps
again, marking his departure with a valedictory
carousal with his cronies. I felt offended that I
should have been included in his boycott for I felt
I had something of the status of a fellow conspira-
tor, apart from being his brother, but his mysterious exit infuriated Mr. Collopy. I never knew quite
why, but I suspected that he had planned a mag-
nanimous farewell, a prayer of God Speed and perhaps the present of one of his prize cutthroat razors.
Mr. Collopy was ever fond of an occasion, and with
encouragement, alike from the company and his
crock, he could attain great heights of eloquence.
The showman in him had been slighted and he was
very offended. He casually asked me whether the
brother could be expected back on a visit for Christmas but I truthfully replied at the time that I had
no idea. Annie seemed to take no notice whatsoever
of this change in our house, even though it meant
less work for her.

About three weeks after the brother's flight, I received a letter from him. It was in a costly long
envelope, in the top left-hand corner of which were
intertwined the letters L.U.A. (I was amused afterwards to notice in an Irish dictionary that *lua*
means "a kick.") The notepaper inside was very
thick and expensive, indeed it was noisy to unfold.
The heading, in black, shining crusted letters, was

LONDON UNIVERSITY ACADEMY, 120 Tooley Street, London, S.W.2. Down along the left margin was a list of the matters in which the Academy offered tuition—Boxing, Foreign Languages, Botany, Poultry Farming, Journalism, Fretwork, Archaeology, Swimming, Elocution, Dietetics, Treatment of High Blood Pressure, Ju-Jutsu, Political Science, Hypnotism, Astronomy, Medicine in the Home, Woodwork, Acrobatics and Wire-Walking, Public Speaking, Music, Care of the Teeth, Egyptology, Slimming, Psychiatry, Oil Prospecting, Railway Engineering, A Cure for Cancer, Treatment of Baldness, La Grande Cuisine, Bridge and Card Games, Field Athletics, Prevention and Treatment of Boils, Laundry Management, Chess, The Vegetable Garden, Sheep Farming, Etching and Drypoint, Sausage Manufacture in the Home, The Ancient Classics, Thaumaturgy Explained, and several other subjects the nature of which I did not understand properly from their names. What corpus of study was alluded to, for instance, in The Three Balls? Or Panpendarism? Or The Cultivation of Sours?

Here was the letter:

"Sorry I could not write before now but I was terribly busy not only settling in at Tooley Street and organizing the office but also meeting people and making contacts. I suppose everybody got a bit of a shock when they found the bird had flown that morning but I could not face a formal farewell with

Collopy puling and puking in the background with
tears of whiskey rolling down his cheeks and gaunt
Father Fahrt giving me his blessings in lordly Latin
and maybe Annie quietly crying into her prashkeen.
You know how I dislike that sort of thing. It makes
me nervous. I'm sorry all the same that I had to be
a bit secretive with yourself but the plans I have
been working on made it essential that Collopy
would know nothing because he has a wonderful
gift for making trouble and poking his nose in
where it will deluge everything with a dirty sneeze.
Did you know that he has a brother in the police at
Henley, not far from here? If he knew my exact
address—which in no circumstances should you
reveal to the bugger—I am sure I would have the
other fellow peering around here, and for all I know
he may be worse than Collopy himself. Needless to
say I did not use any of the addresses the Rev.
Fahrt gave me, for Jesuits can be a far closer police
force than the men in blue. When I get things
more advanced you must come over and give me a
hand because I know this industry I'm entering on
is only in its infancy, that there's bags of money in
it if the business is properly run, and plenty to go
round for everybody. It's a better life here, too. The
pubs are better, food is good and cheap, and the
streets aren't crawling with touchers like Dublin.
Information and help can be got on any subject or
person under the sun for a quid, and often for only
a few drinks.

"Do not pay too much attention to the list of

subjects in the margin. I don't see why we shouldn't
deal with them and plenty more as well, e.g. Religious Vocations, but I am not yet publicly using
this notepaper. You could regard the list in the
margin as a manifesto, a statement of what we intend to do. We really aim at the mass production
of knowledge, human accomplishment and civiliza-
tion. We plan the world of the future, a world of
sophisticated and genial people, all well to do, im-
patient with snivellers, sneaks and politicians on the
make; not really a Utopia but a society in which all
unnecessary wrongs, failures, and misbehaviours are
removed. The simplest way to attack this problem
is to strike at the cause, which is ignorance and non-
education, or miseducation. Every day you meet
people going around with two heads. They are completely puzzled by life, they understand practically
nothing and are certain of only one thing—that
they are going to die. I am not going to go so far as
to contradict them in that but I believe I can sug-
gest to them a few good ways of filling up the interval. A week ago I met a nice class of a negro, apparently a seaman, in a pub in Tower Bridge Road. He
was a gloomy character at first but in three meetings
I taught him to play chess. Now he is delighted
with himself and thinks he is a witch doctor. I also
had a night's drinking with one of the thousands
of ladies who flood the streets here. She wanted me
to go with her but no fear. By her accent I knew she
was Irish; so she was, Castleconnell on the Shan-
non. Same old story about a job as a maid, a tyran-

nical mistress and a young pup of a son that started
pulling her about when she was making the beds.
She came to the conclusion that if that sort of thing
was the custom of the country, she might as well
get paid for it. There is some logic in her argument
but it is painfully clear that she knows next to nothing about business. I talked to her about her mother
and the green hills of Erin and in no time I had her
sniffling, though maybe it was the gin. Those girls
are very fond of that stuff. But don't get the impression that I'm a preacher saving souls every night by
infesting the pubs. It's only an odd night I do that,
and when I'm on my own. I'm far too busy for that
sort of gallivanting. The total staff in the office just
now is four—a typist, a clerk and One Other. The
One Other is my partner, who has put a decent
share of spondulics into the venture. With his
money and my brains, I do not see what there is to
stop us. Better still, he has a well-to-do mother who
lives in a grand house in Hampstead. He does not
live with her or in fact get on with her too well,
apparently because she made him spend two years
at Oxford when he was younger. He says he was
horrified by that place. He signs his name M. B.
Barnes. When I looked for his Christian name—
and you can't have a partner in a new resounding
enterprise without using his Christian name, even
when reprimanding or insulting him—I found that
his full name was Milton Byron Barnes. Maybe this
got him jeered at by the Oxford ignoramuses and
made him sour for life. He is a gloomy type but

knows what work is; and he knows how to talk to people. He is not a poet, of course, but is convinced that his father, long dead, thought *he* was a poet and that he owed it to the masters of the past to commemorate their genius by saddling his unfortunate son with their names. At the moment we are nursing a slight difference between us. He feels one of the fields we must cover is advertising, newspaper and magazine and otherwise. He is convinced that this is the coming thing and keeps quoting High o'er the fence leaps Sunny Jim, FORCE is the food that raises him. He is right that there is big money to be made there but we have not got the capital to wade in—yet. I keep telling him more satisfaction and happiness can be achieved by teaching 10,000 Englishmen to play billiards properly at four guineas for four lessons than by grappling and grovelling in this underground of publicity but his answer is that he does not want to make anybody happy and certainly doesn't want to be happy himself; he just wants to make a lot of money. I find that mentality a bit cynical, but I'm sure I'll bring him round to my own sound views in good time. We had dinner with his old lady twice and I found her quite good and intelligent. I feel it will not be long until she becomes a patron of our Academy and helps it along at important stages with infusions of the red blood of LSD. You know, that is why rich people were made and why we should never envy or insult them. They are people brought into the world armed with the weapons for helping others. Contrast them with Collopy, who spends all his time obstructing and annoying others, poking about to find bad things in order to make them worse, interfering, bickering, and fomenting ill will and fights among friends. More than once I have thought of getting together a course entitled Your Own Business and the Minding of It. I would put Collopy down for free tuition. I'm in digs with another man, an elderly bachelor who owns a tobacco shop and spends his spare time reading Greek. How do I like such company? Very well, for I don't have to buy cigarettes, and the landlady is so old that she occasionally forgets to ask for the rent.

"Keep anything I've said in this note or any other I send under your hat, and don't give anybody in Dublin the firm's address. I'll write soon again. Pass on to me any news that arises. Slip the enclosed pound note with my compliments to Annie. The best of luck."

I sighed and put the letter in my pocket. There was not much in it really.

13

I N the months that followed the weather
was particularly vile: it was a season of downpours
and high wind, and the temperature at night was
such as to compel me to heap two overcoats on top
of my bed. But Mr. Collopy ignored the nightly
tempest. He left the house frequently about eight
and people told me that he was a familiar figure,
sheltering under a sodden umbrella, on the fringe

of the small crowds attending street-corner meetings in Foster Place or the corner of Abbey Street. He was not in any way concerned with the purpose or message of those meetings. He was there to heckle, and solely from the angle of his own mysterious preoccupation. His main demand was that first things should come first. If the meeting advocated a strike in protest against low wages on the railways, he would counter by roaring that the inertia of the Corporation was more scandalous and a far more urgent matter for the country.

One night he came home very thoroughly drenched, and instead of going straight to bed, he sat at the range taking solace from his crock.

—For heaven's sake go to bed, Father, Annie said. You are drownded. Go to bed and I will make you punch.

—Ah no, he said brightly. In such situations my early training as a hurler will stand to me.

Sure enough, he had a roaring cold the following morning and did stay in bed for a few days by command of Annie, who did not lack his own martinet quality. Gradually the cold ebbed but when he was about the house again his movements were very awkward and he complained loudly of pains in his bones. Luckily he was saved the excruciation of trying to go upstairs, for he had himself built a lavatory in the bedroom in Mrs. Crotty's time. But his plight was genuine enough, and I suggested that on my way to school I should drop in a note summoning Dr. Blennerhassett.

—I am afraid, he said, that that good man is day tros. He means well but damn the thing he knows about medicine.

—But he might know something about those pains of yours.

—Oh, all right.

Dr. Blennerhassett did call and said Mr. Collopy had severe rheumatism. He prescribed a medicament which Annie got from the chemist—red pills in a round white box labelled "The Tablets." He also said, I believe, that the patient's intake of sugar should be drastically reduced, that alcohol should not in any circumstances be consumed, that an endeavour should be made to take mild exercise, and to have hot baths as often as possible. Whether or not Mr. Collopy met those four conditions or any of them, he grew steadily worse as the weeks went by. He took to using a stick but I actually had to assist him in the short distance between his armchair and his bed. He was a cripple, and a very irascible one.

I had arranged one night to attend a session of Jack Mulloy's poker school, but a crafty idea had crept into my head. A late start for 8:30 P.M. had been fixed, apparently because Jack had to go somewhere or do something first. I deliberately put my watch an hour fast, and hopefully knocked on the door in nearby Mespil Road at what was really half seven. A pause, and the door was opened by Penelope.

—My, you're early, she said in that charming husky voice.

I gracefully stepped into the hall and said it was nearly half eight. I showed her my watch.

—Your watch is crazy, she said, but come in to the fire. Will you have a cup of coffee?

—I will, Penelope, if you will have one with me.

—I won't be a moment.

Wasn't that a delightful little ruse of mine? So far as I could see, we were alone in the house. Silly ideas came into my head, ideas that need not be mentioned here. I was the veriest tyro in such situations. Into my head came the names of certain voluptuaries and libertines of long ago, and then I began to wonder how the brother would handle matters were he in my place. She came with a pot of coffee, biscuits, and two delightful little cups. In the light her belted dress was trim, modest, a little bit mysterious; or perhaps I mean enchanting.

—Well now, Finbarr, she said, tell me all the news and leave nothing out.

—There's no news.

—I don't believe that, Finbarr. You are hiding something.

—Honestly, Penelope.

—How is Annie?

—Annie's in good order. She never changes. In fact she never changes even her clothes. But poor Mr. Collopy is crucified with rheumatism. He is a complete wreck, helpless and very angry with him-

self. He kept going out to get drowned in the rain
every night a few months ago, and this is the price
of him.

—Ah, the poor man.

—And what about poor me? I have to act the
male nurse while I'm in the house.

—Well, everybody needs help some time or other.
You might grow to be a helpless old man yourself.
How would you like that?

—I wouldn't fancy it. Probably I'd stick my head
in the gas oven.

—But if you had very bad rheumatism you
couldn't do that. You wouldn't be able to stoop or
bend.

—Couldn't I get you to call and help me to get
my head in?

—Ah no, Finbarr, that would not be a nice thing.
But I would call all right.

—To do what?

—To nurse you.

—Heavens, that would be very nice.

She laughed. I must have allowed true feeling to
well up in that remark. I certainly meant what I
said, but did not like to appear too brash.

—Do you mean to say, I smiled, that I would
have to have a painful and loathsome disease before you would call to see me?

—Oh, not at all, Finbarr, she said. But I'd be
afraid of Mr. Collopy. He once called me "an un-
mannerly schoolgirl," all because I told him in the
street that his shoelaces were undone.

—His bootlaces, you mean, I corrected. To hell with Mr. Collopy.

—Now, now, now.

—Well, he gets on my nerves.

—You spend too much time in that kitchen. You don't go out enough. Do you ever go to a dance?

—No. I don't know the first thing about dancing

—That's a pity. I must teach you.

—That would be grand.

—But first we'd have to get the loan of a gramophone somewhere.

—I think I might manage that.

Our conversation, as may be seen, was trivial and pointless enough, and the rest of it was that kind.

Finally I got a bit bolder and took her hand in my own. She did not withdraw it.

—What would you do, I asked, if I were to kiss your hand?

—Well, well! I would scream the house down, probably.

—But why?

—That's the why.

Uproar ensued all right, but it was in the hall. Jack Mulloy with two other butties had come in and were jabbering loudly as they hung up their coats. Alas, I had to disengage my excited mind and turn my thought to cards.

Curiously, I won fifteen shillings that night and was reasonably cheerful over the whole evening's proceedings, not excluding the little interlude with Penelope, as I made my way home. The route I

took was by Wilton Place, a triangular shaded nook
not much used by traffic. I knew from other experiences that it was haunted by prostitutes of the very
lowest cadres, and also by their scruffy clients. A
small loutish group of five or six people were gig-
gling in the shadows as I approached but became
discreetly silent as I passed. But when I had gone
only two yards or so, I heard one solitary word in a
voice I swore I knew:

—*Seemingly.*

I paused involuntarily, deeply shocked, but I
soon walked on. I had, in fact, been thinking of
Penelope, and that one word threw my mind into a
whirl. What was the meaning of this thing sex,
what was the nature of sexual attraction? Was it all
bad and dangerous? What was Annie doing late at
night, standing in a dark place with young black-
guards? Was I any better myself in my conduct,
whispering sly things into the ear of lovely and innocent Penelope? Had I, in fact, at the bottom of
my heart dirty intentions, some dark deed post-
poned only because the opportunity had not yet
presented itself?

As I had expected, the kitchen was empty, for I
had assisted Mr. Collopy to bed before going out
earlier. I did not want to be there when Annie
came. I got notepaper and an envelope, went upstairs and got into bed.

I lay there with the light on for a long time, reflecting. Then I wrote a confidential and detailed
letter to the brother about, first, the very low and

painful condition of Mr. Collopy; and second, the devastating incident concerning Annie. I paused before signing my name and for a wild few minutes considered writing a little about myself and Penelope. But reason, thank God, prevailed. I said nothing but signed and sealed the letter.

14

A REPLY was not long coming, taking the form of a parcel and a letter. I opened the letter first, and here it is:

"Many thanks for your rather alarming communication.

"From what you say it is clear to me that Collopy is suffering from rheumatoid arthritis, very

likely of the periarticular type. If you can persuade
him to let you have a look, you will find that the
joints are swollen and of fusiform shape and I think
you will find that he is afflicted at the hands and
feet, knees, ankles and wrists. Probably his temperature is elevated, and total rest in bed is most desirable. The focus of infection for rheumatoid
arthritis is usually bad teeth and the presence in the
gums of pyorrhoea alveolaris, so that he should
order Hanafin's cab and call on a dentist. But happily we have invented here in the Academy a certain cure for the disorder, provided the treatment is
sedulously followed. I am sending you under sepa-
rate cover a bottle of our patent Gravid Water. It
will be your own job to make sure that he takes
a t/spoonful of it three times a day after meals. See
to the first dose before you leave the house in the
morning, inquire about the daytime dose when
you get back from school, and similarly ensure the
evening dose. It would be well to tell Annie of the
importance of this treatment and the need for
regularity . . ."

At this stage I opened the parcel and under many
wrappings uncovered a large bottle which bore a
rather gaudy label. Here was its message:

THE GRAVID WATER
The miraculous specific for the
complete cure within one
month of the abominable

scourage known as Rheumatoid
Arthritis.
Dose—one t-spoonful three
times daily after meals.
Prepared at
LONDON ACADEMY LABORATORIES

Well, this might be worth trying, I thought, but
immediately soaked the bottle in water and removed the label, for I knew that nothing would
induce Mr. Collopy to touch the contents if he
knew or suspected that they had originated with the
brother. I then resumed reading the letter:

"I was certainly shocked to hear that Annie has
been consorting with cornerboys up the canal.
These are dirty merchants and if she continues,
disease will be inevitable. I am sure that neither
you nor I could attempt any estimate of how cunning and cute she is or how totally ignorant and
innocent. Does she know the Facts of Life? Apart
from venereal disease, does she know of the danger
of pregnancy? I don't think the arrival of an ille-
gitimate on the doorstep would alleviate Collopy's
rheumatoid condition.

"You did not say in your letter that you suspected
that she had some infection but if she has, diagnosis
without examination at this distance is rather difficult. I think we may rule out Granuloma Inguinale.
It takes the form of very red, beefy ulceration. A
clear symptom is ever-increasing debility and

marked physical wasting, often ending in extreme cachexia and death. It is mostly met with in tropical countries, and almost confined to negroes. We may discount it.

"For similar reasons of rarity, we may discard the possibility of Lymphogranuloma Venereum. This is a disease of the lymph glands and lymph nodes, and one finds a hot, painful group of swollen buboes in the inguinal area. There will be headaches, fever and pains in the joints. The causative agent is a virus. Here again, however, Lymphogranuloma Venereum is a near-monopoly of the negro.

"The greatest likelihood is that Annie, if infected, labours under the sway of H.M. Gonococcus. In women the symptoms are so mild at the beginning as to be unnoticed but it is a serious and painful invasion. There is usually fever following infection of the pelvic organs. Complications to guard against include endocarditis, meningitis and skin decay. Gonococcal endocarditis can be fatal.

"There remains, of course, the Main Act. This disease is caused by a virus known as *spirochaeta pallida* or *treponema pallidum*. We can have skin rash, lesions of the mouth, enlargement of lymph glands, loss of scalp hair, inflammation of the eyes, jaundice from liver damage, convulsions, deafness, meningitis and sometimes coma. The Last Act, the most serious, in most cases takes a cardiovascular form where the main lesion is seated in the thoracic aorta directly near the heart. The extensible tissue is ruined, the aorta swells and a saccular dilatation or an aneurysm may take shape. Sudden death is quite common. Other results are G.P.I. (paresis), locomotor ataxia, and wholesale contamination of the body and its several organs. My London Academy Laboratories markets a three-in-one remedy, 'Love's Lullaby,' but as this specific involves fits and head-staggers in persons who have in fact not been infected at all, it would be unwise to prescribe for Annie on the blind.

"I would advise that at this stage you would keep her under very minute observation and see if you can detect any symptoms and then get in touch with me again. You might perhaps devise some prophylactic scheming such as remarking apropos of nothing that conditions on the canal bank are nothing short of a scandal with men and women going about there poxed up to the eyes, drunk on methylated spirits, flooding the walks with contaminated puke and making it unsafe for Christians even to take a walk in that area. You could add that you are writing to the D.M.P. urging the arrest at sight of any characters found loitering there. We all know that probably Annie is a cute and cunning handful but very likely she is not proof against a good fright. On the other hand you might consider telling Mr. Collopy what you know, for it would be easier for a father to talk straight to his own daughter on this very serious subject, on the off-chance that Annie is innocent and quite uninstructed; in fact it would be his duty to do so. If you see fit to adopt that course, it would be natural to bring Father Fahrt into the picture, for the matter has a self-evident spiritual content. If being on the scene you would feel embarrassed to thus take the initiative, I could write from here to Mr. Collopy or Father Fahrt or both, telling of the information I have received (not disclosing the source) and asking that steps should be taken for prevention and/or cure.

"However, I must say that I doubt whether Annie is in trouble at all and the best plan might be to keep wide-awake so far as yourself is concerned, report to me if there are any symptoms or other development, and take no action for the present."

Well, that was a long and rather turgid letter but I found myself in agreement with the last paragraph. In fact I put the whole subject out of my head and merely dedicated myself to Mr. Collopy's rheumatism.

15

I DULY produced the bottle of Gravid
Water to Mr. Collopy, saying it was a miracle cure
for rheumatism which I had got from a chemist
friend. I also produced a tablespoon and told him
he was to take a spoonful without fail three times
a day after meals. And I added that I would keep
reminding him.

—Oh well now, I don't know, he said. Are there salts in it?

—No, I don't think so.

—Is there anything in the line of bromide or saltpetre?

—No. I believe the stuff in the fluid is mostly vitamins. I would say it is mainly a blood tonic.

—Ah-ah? The blood is all, of course. It's like the mainspring on a watch. If a man lets his blood run down, he'll find himself with all classes of boils and rashes. And scabs.

—And rheumatism, I added.

—And who is this chemist when he is at home?

—He's . . . he's a chap I know named Donnelly. He works in Hayes, Conyngham and Robinson. He is a qualified man, of course.

—Oh very well. I'll take a chance. Amn't I nearly crippled? What have I to lose?

—Nothing at all.

There and then he took his first tablespoonful and after a week of the treatment said he felt much better. I was glad of this and emphasized the necessity of persevering in the treatment. From time to time I wrote to the brother for a fresh bottle.

After six weeks I began to notice something strange in the patient's attempts at movement. His walk became most laborious and slow and the floor creaked under him. One night in bed I heard with a start a distant rending crash coming from his bedroom off the kitchen. I hurried down to find him breathless and tangled in the wreckage of his bed.

It seems that the wire mattress, rusted and rotted by Mrs. Crotty's nocturnal diuresis (or bed-wetting) had collapsed under Mr. Collopy's weight.

—Well the dear knows, he said shrilly, isn't this the nice state of affairs? Help me out of this.

I did so, and it was very difficult.

—What happened? I asked.

—Faith and can't you see? The whole shooting-gallery collapsed under me.

—The fire is still going in the kitchen. Put on your overcoat and rest there. I'll take this away and get another bed.

—Very well. That catastrophe has me rightly shaken. I think a dram or two from the crock is called for.

Not in a very good temper, I took down the whole bed and put the pieces against the wall in the passage outside. Then I dismantled the brother's bed and re-erected it in Mr. Collopy's room.

—Your bed awaits, sir, I told him.

—Faith now and that was quick work, he said. I will go in directly I finish this nightcap. You may go back to your own bed.

On the following day, Sunday, I went in next door and borrowed their weighing scales. When I managed to get Mr. Collopy to stand on the little platform, the needle showed his weight to be 406 pounds! I was flabbergasted. I checked the machine by weighing myself and found it was quite accurate. The amazing thing was that Mr. Collopy was still the same size and shape as of old. I could attribute

his extraordinary weight only to the brother's
Gravid Water, so I wrote to him urgently explain-
ing what had happened. And the letter I got back
was surprising enough in itself. Here it is:

"It is not only in Warrington Place that amazing
things are happening; they are happening here as
well. A week ago the mother of Milton Byron
Barnes, my partner, died. In her will, which came
to light yesterday, she left him her house and about
£20,000 in cash and she left £5,000 TO ME! What
do you think of that? It looks like the blessing of
God on my Academy.

"I was indeed sorry about what you tell me of
Mr. Collopy. The cause of it is too obvious—exces-
sive dosage. On the label of the bottle the term
't-spoonful' meant 'tea-spoonful,' not 'tablespoonful.' The Gravid Water, properly administered, was
calculated to bring about a gradual and controlled
increase in weight and thus to cause a redevelop-
ment of the rheumatoid joints by reason of the
superior weight and the increased work they would
have to do.

"Unfortunately the alarming overweight you report is an irreversible result of the Gravid Water;
there is no antidote. In this situation we must put
our trust in God. In humble thanks for my own
legacy and to help poor Mr. Collopy, I have made
up my mind to bring him and Father Fahrt on a
pilgrimage to Rome. The present Pontiff, Pius X,
or Giuseppe Sarto, is a very noble and holy man,

and I do not think it is in the least presumptuous to expect a miracle and have Mr. Collopy restored to his proper weight. Apart from that, the trip will be physically invigorating, for I intend to proceed by sea from London to the port of Ostia in the Mediterranean, only about sixty miles from the Eternal City. Please advise both pilgrims accordingly and tell them to see immediately about passports and packing clothes.

"You should have ingestion of the Gravid Water discontinued and need not disclose the spiritual aim of the pilgrimage to Mr. Collopy. I will write again in a week or so."

16

T<small>HE</small> velocity and efficiency of the brother's methods were not long being made manifest. Before Mr. Collopy had time to bestir himself about the passport, he received out of the blue for completion documents of application for a passport. This was, of course, the brother's doing. Father Fahrt heard nothing; he must already have a passport, else how could he be in Ireland? A few days afterwards I myself received a registered package containing visa application forms to be completed immediately by Mr. Collopy and Father Fahrt and returned to the brother in London. Enclosed also was quite a sum in cash. He wrote:

"See that the visa documents enclosed are signed and returned to me here within forty-eight hours. If Collopy has not yet got his passport fixed up, will you yourself do any running around on his behalf that is necessary and if need be get a photographer *to call to the house.* We leave Tilbury on the *Moravia* in nine days and we don't want things messed up by petty delays or for the sake of saving a few pounds. Tell Father Fahrt that he need have no worry about ecclesiastical permission to travel, as I have had an approach made to the Provincial of the English Jesuits and you may be sure a letter has already gone to the Leeson Street house.

"I have already bought three first-class tickets to the port of Ostia, near Rome. N.B. The Cardinal Archbishop of Ostia is ex officio the Dean of the Sacred College and since our objective is a private audience with the Holy Father, he could be very useful if we could contact him en route. Father Fahrt may have a line on him.

"Dress clothes are essential where an audience is concerned but tell Collopy not to trouble about that. I will have him fixed up with a monkey suit either here in London or when we get to Rome.

"I have booked two adjoining rooms on the first floor of the Hotel Élite et des Étrangers, a big place near the station, and where there is a lift. Father Fahrt will have to look after himself, as these lads are not allowed to stay in hotels. Probably he will stay in the Jesuit house here, or in some convent.

"I enclose one hundred and twenty pounds in notes, being forty pounds each for Collopy and Father Fahrt in respect of the Dublin-London journey, twenty pounds for yourself to meet embarkation expenses, and twenty for Annie to keep her quiet. Tell her to keep away from that canal bank while her dear father is on an important spiritual mission abroad.

"Your plan must be to get Hanafin to drive the party to Westland Row to get the very first boat train to Kingstown on the evening of the seventh. Do not hesitate to tip porters or others heavily to assist Collopy in these difficult moving operations, and if necessary carry him. Arm yourself with a half-pint towards the journey to the boat but tell Father Fahrt to restrain Collopy from any heavy drinking on board, for he probably knows next to nothing about sailing and if he is going to get sick, drink will make the performance all the more atrocious.

"I will meet the party at Euston, with all necessary transport and assistance, early on the morning of the eighth.

"Please attend to all these matters without fail and send me a telegram if there is any holdup."

.   .   .

And so, indeed, it came to pass.

I had privately advised Mr. Collopy to buy two new suits, a heavy one for travel and a light one to meet the Roman weather. He absolutely refused to buy a new overcoat, disinterring an intact but quaint garment in which he said he was married to his first wife. (I had never heard of anyone having been married in an overcoat.) Father Fahrt, being of continental origin, understood everything perfectly and did not need advice on any matter. He did not disguise his emotion at the prospect of meeting the Holy Father in person and referred to this, not as a possibility, but as something which had already been arranged. For all I knew, he had invoked the mysterious apparatus of his Order, from which even the Pope was not immune.

On the late evening of the seventh the two travellers, looking very spruce, were at their accustomed station in the kitchen, savouring refreshment from the crock and looking very pleased. For once Annie showed a slight strain of excitement.

—Could I make you hang sangwiches for the journey? she asked.

—God Almighty, woman, Mr. Collopy said in genuine astonishment, do you think we are going to the zoo? Or Leopardstown races?

—Well, you might be hungry.

—Yes, Mr. Collopy said rather heavily, that could happen. But there is one well-known remedy for hunger. Know what that is? A damn good dinner. Sirloin, roast potatoes, asparagus, Savoy cabbage

and any God's amount of celery sauce. With, be-
forehand, of course, a plate of hot mushroom soup
served with French rolls. With a bottle of claret,
the château class, beside each plate. Am I right,
Father Fahrt?

—Collopy, I don't find that meal very homoge-
neous.

—Maybe so. But is it nourishing?

—Well, it would scarcely kill you.

—Damn sure it never killed me when the mother
was alive. Lord save us—there was a woman that
could bake a farl of wheaten bread! Put a slobber of
honey on that and you had a banquet, man.

—The only creatures who eat sensibly, Father
Fahrt said, are the animals. Nearly all humans over-
eat and kill themselves with food.

—Except in the slums, of course, Mr. Collopy
corrected.

—Ah yes, Father Fahrt said sadly. The curse there
is cheap drink and worse—methylated spirits. God
pity them.

—In a way they have more than we have, they
have constitutions of cast iron.

—Yes, but acid is the enemy of iron. I believe
some of those poor people buy a lot of hair oil. Not
for their heads, of course. They drink it.

—Yes. That reminds me, Father. Hand me your
glass. This isn't hair oil I have here.

While he busied himself with the libations, there
was a knock. I hurried to the door and admitted
Mr. Hanafin.

—Well Fathers above, he beamed as he saw the
pair at the range.

—Evening, Hanafin, Mr. Collopy said. Sit down
there for a minute. Annie, get a glass for Mr. Hanafin.

—So we're off tonight to cross the briny ocean?

—Yes, Mr. Hanafin, Father Fahrt said. We have
important business to attend to on the mainland.

—Yes, Mr. Hanafin, I added, and you have just
four minutes to finish that drink. I am in charge of
this timetable. We all leave for Westland Row
station in four minutes.

My voice was peremptory, stern.

—I must say, gentlemen, Mr. Hanafin said, that
I never seen ye looking better. Ye are very spruce. I
never seen you, Mr. Collopy, with a better colour
up.

—That is my blood pressure, Mr. Collopy replied
facetiously.

I was strict with my four-minute time limit.
When it was up we embarked on the task of getting Mr. Collopy into his ancient tight overcoat.
That completed, Mr. Hanafin and I half-assisted,
half-dragged him out to the cab and succeeded,
Father Fahrt assisting from the far door, in hoisting him into the cab's back. The springs wheezed
as he collapsed backwards on to the seat. Soon after
the aged Marius broke into a leisurely trot and in
fifteen minutes we pulled up outside Westland
Row station. There is a long flight of steps from
street level to the platform.

—Everybody wait here till I come back, I said.

I climbed the stairs and approached a porter standing beside the almost empty boat train.

—Listen here, I said, there's a very heavy man below in a cab that wouldn't be able for those stairs on his own. If you get another man to come down with you and give us a hand, there's a ten bob each for you in it.

His eyes gleamed, he bawled for Mick, and soon the three of us descended. Getting Mr. Collopy out of the cab was more a matter of strategy than strength but soon he was standing breathless and shaky on the pathway.

—Now, Mr. Collopy, I said, those stairs are the devil. There are four of us here and we are going to carry you up.

—Well faith now, Mr. Collopy said mildly. I am told they used to carry the Roman emperors about the Forum in Rome, dressed up in purest cloth of gold.

I posted a porter at each shoulder to grip him by the armpits while Mr. Hanafin and I took charge of a leg apiece, rather as if they were the shafts of a cart. Clearly the porters were deeply shocked at the weight they had to deal with at the rear but we assailed the stairs, trying to keep the passenger as horizontal as possible, and found the passage easy enough. Father Fahrt hurried ahead and opened the door of an empty first-class carriage, and Mr. Collopy was adroitly put standing on the floor. He was very pleased and beamed about him as if he himself had just performed some astonishing feat. Mr. Hanafin hurried down to get the luggage, while I bought the tickets.

It was nearly three-quarters of an hour before the train moved and half an hour before anybody else entered our compartment. I produced a small glass and to his astonishment, handed it to Mr. Collopy. Then I produced a flat half-pint bottle from my hip pocket.

—I have already put a little water into this stuff, I said, so you can have a drink of it with safety.

—Well merciful martyrs in heaven, Father Fahrt, Mr. Collopy said gleefully, did you ever hear the like of it? Drinking whiskey in a first-class carriage and us on a pilgrimage to kneel at the feet of the Holy Father!

—Please do not take much, Father Fahrt said seriously. It is not good to do this in public.

When the train pulled up alongside the mailboat at Kingstown, I repeated my stratagem with the two porters. We got Mr. Collopy comfortably seated, at his own request, in the dining saloon. I felt tired and told him and Father Fahrt that I must be off.

—God bless you for your help, my boy, Father Fahrt said.

—When you get back, Mr. Collopy said, tell Annie that there are two pairs of dirty socks at the bottom of my bed. They want to be washed and darned.

—Right.

—And if Rafferty calls about hydrometer readings, tell him to keep the machine in circulation. Make a note of this. Next on the list is Mrs. Hayes of Sandymount. Next, Mrs. Fitzherbert of Harold's Cross. He knows those people. I'll be home by then.

—Very good. Good-bye now, and good luck.

And so they sailed away. How did they fare? That peculiar story was revealed in dispatches I received from the brother, and which I now present.

17

ABOUT *three weeks after the depar-*
ture of the travellers I received the following letter
from the brother:

Well, here we are in Rome at the Hotel Élite et
des Étrangers. Spring comes earlier here and it is
already very warm.

Our voyage to Ostia on the *Moravia* was without
much incident and for me quite enjoyable. I

haven't been so drunk for years, though an Englishman I chummed up with went a bit further. He fell and broke his leg. Collopy, who never showed any sign of sickness, drank plenty too but spent most of his time in bed. (Thank God we had decent beds and not those frightful bunks.) First, the job of trying to dress him on a tilting floor was at least an hour's for Father Fahrt, a steward and myself. Once dressed, he found movement on shipboard almost impossible. I had to give another steward not tips but a massive salary to lend a special hand, but gangways and steps were nearly insuperable. I used to bring people down to the bedroom to drink and talk with him. He was not in the least depressed by his situation, and the sea air certainly had a good effect. Father Fahrt rather let us down. He soon found there were four members of his own Order on board and was huddled with them for most of every day. He came down to Collopy only in the evening, and for some reason has refused all drinks. He is in very good shape and temper, though, and is now staying in a Jesuit house here. He comes faithfully to the hotel every morning at eleven.

Collopy is much easier to handle and dress on terra firma—indeed, he could dress himself if he was using the tramp's rags he wears in Dublin—and we usually spend the first part of the day till lunch time sitting in the sun and talking. Irish whiskey is impossible to get, of course, and Collopy is drinking absinthe. I am drinking so much brandy myself that I sometimes get afraid of heart failure. In the afternoons we usually hire a wagonette and go for a slow tour of sights such as the Colosseum and the Forum; we have been twice to the piazza of Saint Peter's. At night, I see Collopy put to bed and just disappear until the small hours. I find the Eternal City is full of brothels but I keep clear of them. There are some damn fine night clubs, most of them, I am told, illegal.

And now for the inside trickery. I knew we could rely on Father Fahrt to start secret schemings without even being asked. Yesterday morning he brought along a Monsignor Cahill, a remarkable character and a Corkman. He is a sort of Vatican civil servant and attends on the Holy Father personally. He is not only an interpreter who has expert knowledge of at least eight languages (he says) but he is also a stenographer whose job it is to take down all remarks and observations made by the Holy Father in the course of an audience. He translates the supplications of pilgrims orally but takes down only the replies. He is a most friendly man, is always genuinely delighted to see anybody from Ireland, and knows exactly what to do with a good glass of wine. He took a great fancy to Collopy who, to my own great surprise, has a detailed knowledge of Cork city.

He promised to do everything possible to arrange a private audience but Father Fahrt has a far bigger card in his pack. He knows, or has made it his business to get to know, a certain Cardinal Baldini. This man is what they call a domestic prelate, and works every day in the papal suite. He has, of course, enormous power and can fix anything. Father Fahrt is very cagey and has promised Collopy nothing solid beyond saying that the Pontiff is very busy and one must be patient. Personally I have no doubt at all that this audience will come off. I believe in it sufficiently to have bought Collopy a monkey suit. Cardinal Baldini is a Franciscan and lives at the Franciscan monastery at the Via Merulana, where there is also the fine church of Santo Antonio di Padua. (My Italian is improving fast.) That is all for now. Will write again in a few days.—M.

P.S. Keep your eye on Annie. I hope there is no canal nonsense going on.

18

THE *next letter I received was a short
one, a week afterwards. Here is what he wrote:*

Well, the expected happened. Father Fahrt came
as usual this morning and after some small talk,
casually told Collopy and myself to have our monkey suits on that evening at six because we were all
going to pay a call on Cardinal Baldini at his monastery. It was a most dramatic revelation. Obvi-

ously Father Fahrt had been working quietly and silently behind the scenes, in the Jesuit fashion. I knew the private audience had been fixed but said nothing.

Having first fixed myself up, I took the precaution of beginning the job of getting Collopy into his dress clothes at five and it was a wise move, for it took nearly an hour. He looked very funny in the end.

We drove with Father Fahrt to the Via Merulana. The monastery was a simple, austere place but apparently very big. The reception room was comfortable enough but full of holy pictures. Cardinal Baldini when he came in was a short, stout man, very jovial in manner. We kissed his ring as he greeted us in perfect English. We sat down at our ease.

"And how are all my friends in Dublin?" he asked Collopy.

"Faith and they are in very good form, your Eminence. I did not know you were there."

"I paid a visit in 1896. And I spent ten years in England."

"Well, well."

Then Father Fahrt started yapping out of him about the charm of foreign travel, how it broadens the mind and shows the Catholic how universal the universal Church is.

"I was never one to roam," Collopy said. "Somehow a man must stay where his work is."

"True indeed," Cardinal Baldini said, "but our

vineyard is indeed commodious. And every year that passes it gets bigger. Look at the work that is yet to be done in Africa, in China, even in Japan."

"I realize how immense the job is," Collopy replied, "because I have been doing missionary work of my own. Not the religious kind, of course."

Here Father Fahrt began talking about the central point of all religion—the Vatican and the Holy Father.

Finally, the Cardinal turned to Collopy and said:

"Mr. Collopy, I believe yourself and your little party would like to have a private audience with the Holy Father?"

"Your Eminence, it would be indeed a great honour."

"Well, I have arranged it. The afternoon of the day after tomorrow at four o'clock."

"We are all most grateful to you, Eminence," Father Fahrt said.

That was about all. We drove back to the hotel very pleased with ourselves. I went straight to the American bar there to celebrate. The audience will be over by the time you get this. I will write immediately and give you an account of it.—M.

19

I MUST *let the next extraordinary letter speak for itself. It put the heart across me.*

Several days have passed since that audience and it is only now that I am able, with Monsignor Cahill's help, to send you this letter. Please keep it safely as I have no copy.

There was a frightful, appalling row.

As a matter of fact the Pope told us all to go to hell. He threatened to silence Father Fahrt.

The papal palaces are to the right of the basilica as you approach it and just past the entrance, Father Fahrt led us to a small office run by the Swiss Guards. It was a private rendezvous, for in five minutes Cardinal Baldini appeared, welcomed us and gave each of us a thick guide or catalogue. As there was plenty of time to spare, he led us through this enormous and dazzling place talking all the time, showing us the loggia of Gregory XIII, a wonderful gallery; the Throne Room; the Sala Rotunda, a round hall full of statues; the Raphael salon, with many of the great man's paintings; part of the Vatican Museum; the Sistine Chapel and many other places I cannot remember, nor can I remember much from the Cardinal's stream of talk except that the Vatican has a parish priest (not the Pope). The splendour of it all was stupendous. God forgive me, I thought it was a bit vulgar in places and that all the gilt and gold was sometimes a bit overdone.

"The late Leo," Cardinal Baldini said, "was at home with kings and princes and rejoiced in art and the higher learning. Of course his *Rerum Novarum* was a great thing for the labouring classes. But the man you are going to meet is the Pope of the poor and the humble. In any way he can help them, he always does."

"Is that a fact?" Collopy said.

I thought of the miracle we were hoping for concerning his weight. But he had yet been told nothing of that.

We came to a door and entered a beautiful room. This was the anteroom to the Pope's study. The Cardinal bade us wait and passed through another door. The place was delightfully peaceful. After some minutes the other door opened and the Cardinal beckoned to us. We allowed Collopy, slowly progressing on his stick, to lead the way, myself in the middle and Father Fahrt last.

The Holy Father was seated behind a desk, with Monsignor Cahill sitting some distance to his right. Pius X was smallish, rather thin and looked fairly old. He smiled thinly at us, rose and came round to meet us. We knelt, kissed the Fisherman's Ring and heard his voice raised in Latin as he imparted what I suppose was the apostolic benediction.

He then went back to his seat behind the desk while the pilgrims and the Cardinal advanced to chairs facing it. I chose a chair far to the side, for I did not want to make any remarks or have any questions addressed to me. I noticed that Monsignor Cahill had paper and a pencil ready.

The Pope said something in Italian to Mr. Collopy and Monsignor Cahill instantly translated, also rapidly translating his reply back into Italian.

THE POPE—How do things fare in your country, beloved Ireland?

COLLOPY—Only middling, your Holiness. The British are still there.

THE POPE—And is the country not prosperous?

COLLOPY—I do not think so, your Holiness, for there is much unemployment in Dublin.

THE POPE—Ah, that grieves our heart.

FATHER FAHRT (in Italian)—Some of the Irish tend to be a bit indolent, Sanctissime Pater, but their faith is perhaps the strongest in Christendom. I am a German and have seen nothing like it in Germany. It is inspiring.

THE POPE—Ireland was ever dear to our heart. She is a blessed country. Her missionaries are everywhere.

(After a little more desultory conversation Mr. Collopy said something in a low voice which I did not catch. Monsignor Cahill instantly translated. The Pope seemed startled. Mr. Collopy then made a much longer mumbled speech which was also quickly translated. I am indebted to Monsignor Cahill for a transcription of the Pope's remarks, which were in Latin and Italian, and the translation is also largely his.)

COLLOPY spoke.

THE POPE

Che cosa sta dicendo questo poveretto?

What is this poor child trying to say?

MONSIGNOR CAHILL spoke.

THE POPE

E tocco? Nonnunquam urbis nostrae visitentium

capitibus affert vaporem. Dei praesidium hujus infantis amantissimi invocare velimus.

Is this child in his senses? Sometimes the heat of our city brings a vapour into the heads. We invoke God's protection for a beloved child.

COLLOPY spoke again.

MONSIGNOR CAHILL spoke.

THE POPE

Ho paura che abbiate fatto un errore, Eminenza, nel portar qui questo pio uomo. Mi sembra che sia un po' tocco. Forse gli manca una rotella. Ha sbagliato indirizzo? Non siamo medici che curano il corpo.

Dear Cardinal, I fear you have made a mistake in bringing this pious man to see us. I fear the Lord has laid a finger on him. We would not say that his head is working properly. Can it be that he is at the wrong place? We are not a doctor for the body.

FATHER FAHRT spoke.

THE POPE

Ma questo è semplicemente mostruoso. Neque hoc nostrum officium cum concilii urbani officio est confundendum.

But this is monstrous. Nor should our office be confused with that of a city council.

CARDINAL BALDINI spoke.

THE POPE

Nobis presentibus istud dici indignum est. Num consilium istud inusitatum rationis legibus con-

tinetur? Nunquam nos ejusmodi quicquam audivi-
mus.
It is a derogation of our presence. Does such an
unheard-of suggestion lie within reason? We have
never heard of such a thing before.

COLLOPY mumbled something.
MONSIGNOR CAHILL spoke.
THE POPE
Graviter commovemur ista tam mira observa-
tione ut de tanta re sententiam dicamus. Intra hos
parietes dici dedecet. Hic enim est locus sacer.
We are deeply troubled by such a strange sup-
plication for our intervention on such a question.
It is improper that such a matter should be men-
tioned within these walls. This is a sacred place.

CARDINAL BALDINI spoke in Italian.
THE POPE
Non possiamo accettare scuse e pretesti. Il Rev-
erendo Fahrt ha sbagliato. Ci da grande dolore.
We cannot accept pretexts and excuses. Father
Fahrt has lapsed. He fills us with sorrow.

FATHER FAHRT spoke in Italian.
THE POPE
Non possiamo accetare ciò. Sembra ci sia un
rilassamento nella disciplina nella Società di Gesù
in Irlanda. Se il Padre Provinciale non agisce,
dovremo noi stessi far tacere il Reverendo Fahrt.
We do not accept that at all. There seems to be

a weakness of discipline in the Society of Jesus in Ireland. If Father Provincial in Ireland does not move, we will silence Father Fahrt ourselves.

COLLOPY mumbled something.

MONSIGNOR CAHILL spoke.

CARDINAL BALDINI spoke in Italian.

THE POPE

È inutile parlarne. Quest' uomo soffre di allucinazioni di ossessioni, ed e stato condotto su questa via del Reverendo Fahrt. Come abbiamo già detto, tutto questo ci rattrista profondamente, Cardinale.

It is no good. This man is suffering from serious delusions and obsessions and he is being encouraged in this disorder by Father Fahrt. As we have said, it brings sorrow to our heart, Cardinal.

CARDINAL BALDINI spoke.

THE POPE

Homo miserrimus in valetudinario a medico curandus est.

This poor man needs attention in hospital.

CARDINAL BALDINI spoke again.

THE POPE

Bona mulier fons gratiae. Attamen ipsae in parvularum rerum suarum occupationibus verrentur. Nos de tantulis rebus consulere non decet.

A good woman is a fountain of grace. But it is themselves whom they should busy about their private little affairs. It is not seemly to consult us on such matters.

CARDINAL BALDINI spoke yet again.

THE POPE

Forsitan poena leviora ille Reverendus Fahrt adduci possit ut et sui sit memor et quae sacerdotis sint partes intellegere.

Perhaps a milder penance will bring Father Fahrt to recollect himself and have true regard to his holy duties.

The Pope then rose and the members of the audience also rose.

THE POPE

Nobis nunc abeundum esse videtur. Illud modo ex liberis meis quaero ut de iis cogiteat quae exposui.

I think we should now retire. I ask my children to meditate upon the thoughts we have voiced.

The Holy Father then made the Sign of the Cross, and disappeared through a door behind him.

We silently filed out through the anteroom, Cardinal Baldini walking ahead with Father Fahrt, the two of them talking together quietly. At the time I had no idea, of course, what the subject of the audience had been or what had been said in Latin or Italian by the Pope. It was only when I interviewed Monsignor Cahill the following day that I got the information I have set down here. I asked him what the *subject* of Mr. Collopy's representations were. He said he had given his word of honour that he would not disclose this to anybody.

My progress at Mr. Collopy's side in the Vatican corridors was slow and tedious. No miracle had cured his fabulous weight. I suppose there was still time.—M.

20

I WAS lying in bed one morning, having already decided I would not go to school that day and thinking that perhaps I would never go back to it. The brother's last extraordinary letter about the Holy Father and Father Fahrt had contained a cheque for twenty-five pounds. I had already trained Annie to bring me some breakfast in bed and was lying there at my ease, smoking and thinking. I could hear men shouting at horses on the tow-path, hauling a barge. It was amazing how quickly life changed. The brother's legacy of £5,000 was a miracle in itself, and another miracle was his feat in founding a new sort of university in London. Then you had the three of them inside the Vatican argu-ing with the Holy Father himself. It would not sur-prise me if the brother turned out to be appointed Governor of Rome or even came home in the pur-ple of a cardinal, for I knew that in the old days it was common for Popes to appoint mere children to be cardinals. I thought I would join the brother in London. Even if his business did not suit me, there would be plenty of other jobs to be had there. Sud-denly Annie came into the room and handed me an orange envelope. It was a cablegram.

COLLOPY DEAD AND FUNERAL IS
TOMORROW HERE IN ROME AM WRITING

I nearly fell out of the bed. Annie stood staring at me.

—Seemingly they are on their way home? she asked.

—Em, yes, I stammered. They will probably take the short route home direct to London. The brother's business, you know.

—Isn't it well for them, she said, to be globe-trot-ting and gallivanting?

—It can be very tiring.

—Ah yes, but look at the money they have. Isn't it well for them?

She went away and I lay there, quite desolated—
I who had been reflecting on the amazing sudden-
ness with which life changed. I had lied auto-
matically to Annie and only now realized that the
dead man was her father. I lit another cigarette and
realized that I had no idea what I should do. What
could I do?

After a time I got up and hung disconsolately
about the house for a time. Annie had gone out,
presumably to buy food. I was completely in a
quandary about breaking the bad news to her. How
would she take it? That question was quite beyond
me. I thought a couple of good bottles of stout
would do me no harm. I was about to pull on my
overcoat when I paused, pulled out the cable again
and stared at it. Then I did what I suppose was
something cowardly. I put the thing on the kitchen
table and walked quickly out of the house. I
crossed over the canal at Baggot Street Bridge and
was soon sitting in a pub looking at a bottle of
stout.

I was not yet really in the habit of heavy drinking but this time I was there for many, many hours
trying desperately to think clearly. I had not much
success. When I did leave it was nearly three o'clock
and I had six stouts under my arm when I stag-
gered home.

There was nobody there. The cablegram was
gone and in its place a note saying THERE IS SOME-
THING IN THE OVEN. I found a chop and some other
things and began to eat. Annie had friends of her

own and probably had gone to one of them. It was just as well. I felt enormously heavy and sleepy. Carefully gathering my stouts, a glass and a corkscrew, I went up to bed and soon fell headlong into a deep, sodden sleep. It was early morning when I awoke. I pulled a stout and lit a cigarette. Gradually, the affairs of the preceding day came back to me.

When Annie arrived with breakfast (for which I had little taste) her eyes were very red. She had been crying a lot but she was collected and calm.

—I am very sorry, Annie, I said.

—Why did they not bring him home to bury him here with my mother?

—I do not know. I am waiting for a letter.

—How well they wouldn't think even of me.

—I am sure they did the best they could in the circumstances.

—Seemingly.

The next three or four days were very grim. There was almost total silence in the house. Neither of us could think of anything to say. I went out a bit and drank some stout but not much. In the end a letter did arrive from the brother. This is what he had to say:

"My cablegram must have been a great shock to you, to say nothing of Annie. Let me tell you what happened.

"After the Vatican rumpus, Father Fahrt and Collopy, but particularly Collopy, were very depressed. I was busy thinking about getting back to London and my business. Father Fahrt thought that some distraction and uplift were called for and booked two seats for a violin recital in a small hall near the hotel. He foolishly booked the most expensive seats without making sure they were not in an upstairs gallery. They were, and approached by a narrow wooden stairs. This concert was in the afternoon. Halfway up the first flight of stairs there was a small landing. Collopy painfully led the way up with his stick and the aid of the banister, Father Fahrt keeping behind to save him if he overbalanced and fell backwards. When Collopy got to this landing and stepped on to the middle of it, there was a rending, splintering crash, the whole floor collapsed and with a terrible shriek, Collopy disappeared through the gaping hole. There was a sickening thud and more noise of breakage as he hit bottom. Poor Father Fahrt was distracted, rushed down, alerted the doorman, got the manager and other people and had a message sent to me at the hotel.

"When I arrived the scene was grotesque. There was apparently no access to the space under the stairs and two carpenters using hatchets, saws and chisels were carefully breaking down the woodwork in the hallway below the landing. About a dozen lighted candles were in readiness on one of the steps, casting a ghastly light on the very shaken Father Fahrt, two gendarmes, a man with a bag who was evidently a doctor and a whole mob of sundry characters, many of them no doubt on-lookers who had no business there.

"The carpenters eventually broke through and pulled away several boards as ambulance men arrived with a stretcher. The doctor and Father Fahrt pushed their way to the aperture. Apparently Collopy was lying on his back covered with broken timbers and plastering, one leg doubled under him and blood pouring from one of his ears. He was semiconscious and groaning pitifully. The doctor gave him some massive injection and then Father Fahrt knelt beside him, and hoarse, faltering whispers told us he was hearing a confession. Then, under the shattered stairway of this cheap Roman hall, Father Fahrt administered the Last Rites to Collopy.

"Getting the unfortunate man on the stretcher after the doctor had given him another knockout injection was an enormous job for the ambulance men, who had to call for assistance from two by-standers. Nobody could understand his prodigious weight. (N.B.—I have changed the label on the Gravid Water bottle to guard strictly against over-dosage.) It was fully twenty minutes before Collopy, now quite unconscious, could be got from under the stairs, and four men were manning the stretcher. He was driven off to hospital.

"Father Fahrt and I walked glumly back to the hotel. He told me he was sure the fall would kill Collopy. After an hour or so he got a telephone call from the hospital. A doctor told him that Collopy was dead on admission, from multiple injuries. He, the doctor, would like to see us urgently and would call to the hotel about six.

"When he arrived, he and Father Fahrt had a long conversation in Italian one word of which, I need hardly say, I did not understand.

"When he had gone, Father Fahrt told me the facts. Collopy had a fractured skull, a broken arm and leg and severe rupture of the whole stomach region. Even if none of those injuries was individually fatal, no man of Collopy's age could survive the shock of such an accident. But what had completely puzzled the doctor and his colleagues was the instantaneous onset of decomposition in the body and its extraordinarily rapid development. The hospital had got in touch with the city health authorities, who feared some strange foreign disease and had ordered that the body be buried the next morning. The hospital had arranged for undertakers to attend, at our expense, the following morning at 10 A.M. and a grave had been booked at the cemetery of Campo Verano.

"I was interested in that mention of premature and rapid decomposition of the body. I am not sure but I would say that here was the Gravid Water again. I said nothing, of course.

"We were early enough at the hospital. Collopy had already been coffined, and a hearse with horses, and a solitary cab, were waiting. I saw the Director and gave him a cheque to cover everything. Then we started out for the church of San

Lorenzo Fuori le Mura, near the cemetery, where Father Fahrt said Requiem Mass. The burial afterwards was indeed a simple affair, for myself and the good priest were the only mourners, and it was he who said the prayers at the graveside.

"We drove back in the cab to the hotel in silence. Father Fahrt had told me that Collopy had made a will and that it was in possession of a Dublin firm of solicitors named Sproule, Higgins and Fogarty. I will have to see those people. In the cab I made up my mind to go home immediately to Dublin, then to London, giving Father Fahrt some money and letting him fend for himself. You will see me almost as soon as you get this letter."

Well, that was the brother's last communiqué from the Continent. And I did see him, two days later.

21

T HE brother walked in unannounced about three-thirty in the afternoon. Thank God Annie was out. He threw his coat and hat on the kitchen table, nodded affably and sat down opposite me at the range in Mr. Collopy's ramshackle old chair.

—Well, he said briskly, and how are we?

He was very well dressed but I concluded he was half drunk.

—We are fair to middling, I said, but that business in Rome has my nerves shattered. You seem to be bearing up pretty well yourself.

—Oh, one has to take these things, he said, making a pouting gesture with his mouth. Nobody will mourn much for us when we go for the long jump and don't fool yourself that they will.

—I liked the poor old man. He wasn't the worst.

—All right. His death wasn't the happiest he could get. In fact it was ridiculous. But look at it this way. In what better place could a man die than in Rome, the Eternal City, by the side of Saint Peter?

—Yes, I said wryly. There was timber concerned in both cases. Saint Peter was crucified.

—Ah, true enough. I have often wondered how exactly crucifixions were carried out in practice. Did they crucify a man horizontally with the cross lying on the ground and then hoist him upright?

—I don't know but I suppose so.

—Well by Gob they would have a job hoisting Collopy up. I am sure that man weighed at least 490 pounds at the end and sure he wasn't anything like the size of you or myself.

—Have you no compunction about your Gravid Water?

—Not at all. I think his metabolism went astray. But anybody who takes patent medicines runs a calculated risk.

—Was Mr. Collopy the first the Gravid Water was tried on?

—I would have to look that up. Look, get two glasses and a sup of water. I've a little drop here before we go out.

He produced a half-pint bottle which was one-third full. I got the glasses, he divided the whiskey and there we were, our glasses on the range and sitting vis-à-vis, for all the world as if we were Mr. Collopy and Father Fahrt. I asked him how Father Fahrt was.

—He is still in Rome, of course. He is in a very morbid state but tries hard at this business of pious resignation. I think he has forgotten about the Pope's threats. I'm sure they were all bluff, anyway. And how's our friend Annie?

—She seems resigned, too. I told her what you said about the necessity for hasty burial. She seemed to accept it. Of course, I said nothing about the Gravid Water.

—Just as well. Here's luck!

—G'luck!

—I rang up those solicitors Sproule, Higgins and Fogarty and made an appointment for half four this evening. We'd better get out now and have a drink first.

—All right.

We took a tram to Merrion Square and went into a pub in Lincoln Place.

—Two balls of malt, the brother ordered.

—No, I interposed. Mine is a bottle of stout.

He looked at me incredulously and then reluctantly ordered a stout.

—In our game, he said, it doesn't do to be seen drinking stout or anything of that kind. People would take you for a cabman.

—I might be that yet.

—Oh, there is one thing I forgot to tell you. On the night before the funeral I got in touch with one of those monumental sculpture fellows and ordered a simple headstone to be ready not later than the following night. I paid handsomely for it and the job was done. It was erected the following morning and I have paid for kerbing to be carried out as soon as the grave settles.

—You certainly think of everything, I said in some admiration.

—Why wouldn't I think of that? I might never be in Rome again.

—Still . . .

—I believe you are a bit of a literary man.

—Do you mean the prize I got for my piece about Cardinal Newman?

—Well, that and other things. You have heard of Keats, of course?

—Of course. *Ode to a Grecian Urn. Ode to Autumn.*

—Exactly. Do you know where he died?

—I don't. In his bed, I suppose?

—Like Collopy, he died in Rome and he is buried

there. I saw his grave. Mick, give us a ball of malt
and a bottle of stout. It is beautiful and very well
kept.

—That is very interesting.

—He wrote his own epitaph. He had a poor opinion of his standing as a poet and wrote a sort of a
jeer at himself on his tombstone. Of course it may
have been all cod, just looking for praise.

—What's this the phrase was?

—He wrote: *Here lies one whose name is writ on
water.* Very poetical, ah?

—Yes, I remember it now.

—Wait till I show you. Drink up that, for goodness' sake! I took a photograph of Collopy's grave
just before I left. Wait till you see now.

He rummaged in his inside pocket and produced
his wallet and fished a photograph out of it. He
handed it to me proudly. It showed a large plain
mortuary slab bearing this inscription:

✠

COLLOPY

of Dublin

1832–1904

Here lies one whose name
is writ in water

R.I.P.

—Isn't it good? he chuckled. "In water" instead
of "on water"?

—Where's his Christian name? I asked.

—Bedammit but I didn't know it. Neither did Father Fahrt.

—Well, where did you get the year of his birth?

—Well, that was more or less a guess. The hospital people said he was a man of about seventy-two, and that's what the doctor has on the death certificate which I have in my pocket. So I just subtracted. What do you think of the stone?

—My turn to buy a drink. What will you have?

—Ball of malt.

I ordered another drink.

—I think the stone looks very well, I said, and you showed great foresight in providing it. I think you should stake out Annie on a trip to her father's grave.

—A very good idea, he said. Excellent.

—We had better finish up here and keep that appointment.

We were slightly late arriving at the office of Sproule, Higgins and Fogarty. A bleak male clerk took our names and went into a room marked MR. SPROULE. He then beckoned us in. Mr. Sproule was an ancient wrinkled thing like his own parchments, remarkably like a character out of Dickens. He rose to a stooped standing and shook hands with us, waving us to chairs.

—Ah, he said, wasn't it sad about poor Mr. Collopy?

—You got my letter from Rome, Mr. Sproule? the brother said.

—I did indeed. We have a correspondent of our

own in Rome, too, the only firm in Dublin with one. We have a lot of work with the Orders.

—Yes, the brother said. We would like to have some idea of what's in the will. Here, by the way, is the death certificate.

—That will be very useful indeed. Thank you. Now I have the will here. I'm sure you don't want to be troubled with all the legalistic rigmarole we lawyers must insist on.

—No, Mr. Sproule, I said impatiently.

—Well, we don't know the exact value of the estate because it consists mostly of investments. But I will summarize the testator's wishes. First, there are capital bequests. The house at Warrington Place he leaves to his daughter Annie, with a thousand pounds in cash. To each of his two half-nephews—and that is you gentlemen—he leaves five hundred pounds in cash provided each is in residence with him in his house at the date of his death.

—Great Lord, the brother cried, that lets me out! I haven't been living there for months.

—That is most unfortunate, Mr. Sproule said.

—And me that's after burying him in Rome and raising a headstone to his memory, all out of my own pocket!

He looked to each of us incredulously.

—That can't be helped, I said severely. What else is there, Mr. Sproule?

—After all that has been done, Mr. Sproule went on, we have to set up the Collopy Trust. The Trust will pay the daughter Annie three hundred pounds a year for life. The Trust will erect and maintain three establishments which the testator calls rest rooms. There will be a rest room at Irishtown, at Sandymount, at Harold's Cross and at Phibsborough. Each will bear the word PEACE very prominently on the door and each will be under the patronage of a saint—Saint Patrick, Saint Jerome and Saint Ignatius. Each of these establishments will bear a plaque reading, for instance, "THE COLLOPY TRUST—Rest Room of Saint Jerome." You will note that they are very well dispersed, geographically.

—Yes indeed, I said. Who is going to design those buildings?

—My dear sir, Mr. Collopy thought of everything. That has already been done. Architect's approved plans are lodged with me.

—Well, is that the lot? the brother asked.

—Substantially, yes. There are a few small bequests and a sum for Masses in favour of Rev. Kurt Fahrt, S.J. Of course, nothing can be paid until the will is admitted to probate. But I take it that will be automatic.

—Very good, I said. My brother lives in London but I am still here. At the old address.

—Excellent. I can write to you.

We turned to go. Abruptly the brother turned at the door.

—Mr. Sproule, he said, may I ask you a question?

—A question? Certainly.

—What was Mr. Collopy's Christian name?

—What?

Mr. Sproule was clearly startled.

—Ferdinand, of course.

—Thanks.

When we found ourselves again in the street, I found that the brother was not as downcast as I thought he might be.

—Ferdinand? Fancy! What I need badly at this moment, he said, is a drink. I am five hundred pounds poorer since I went into that office.

—Well, let us have a drink to celebrate that I'm better off.

—Right. I want to keep near the Kingstown tram, for I'm going to jump the boat tonight. I left my bags in London on the way here. This place will do.

He led the way into a public house in Suffolk Street and to my surprise agreed to drink half-ones instead of balls of malt, in view of the long night's travelling he had to face. He was in a reminiscent, nostalgic mood, and talked of many things in our past lives.

—Have you made up your mind, he asked eventually, what you're going to do with yourself?

—No, I said, except that I have decided to pack up school.

—Good man.

—As regards making a living, I suppose that five hundred pounds will give me at least another two years to think about it if I need all that time.

—Would you not join me at the university in London?

—Well, I'll consider that. But I have a terrible feeling that sooner or later the police will take a hand in that foundation.

—Nonsense!

—I don't know. I feel the ice is pretty thin, smart and all as you are.

—I haven't put a foot wrong yet. Have you ever thought about getting into this new motor business? It's now a very big thing on the other side.

—No, I never thought much about that. I would need capital. Besides, I know nothing whatever about machines. For all the good those damned Brothers have been to me, I know nothing about anything.

—Well, I was the same. The only way to learn anything is to teach yourself.

—I suppose so.

—Tell me this, the brother said rather broodily, how is Annie and how do you get on with her?

—Annie is all right, I said. She is recovering from that terrible affair in Rome. I think she feels grateful to yourself for what you did, though she doesn't talk about it. Do you know what? It would be a nice thing if you gave her a present of a hundred pounds to keep the house and everything going until the will is fixed up.

—Yes, that is a good idea. I'll post a cheque from London and write her a nice letter.

—Thanks.

—Tell me: does she look after you all right?

—Perfectly.

—Grub, laundry, socks and all that?

—Of course. I live like a lord. Breakfast in bed if you please.

—That's good. Lord, look at the time! I'll have to look slippy if I'm to get that boat. Yes, I'm very pleased that Annie is turning out like that. She is a goodhearted girl.

—But what are you talking about? I said rather puzzled. Hasn't she been looking after a whole houseful all her life? Poor Mrs. Crotty in her day never did a hand's turn. She was nearly always sick and, God rest the dead, but Mr. Collopy was a handful in himself, always asking whether there was starch in his food, no matter what you gave him. He even suspected the water in the tap.

—Ah yes. All the same, he paid his debt. I was delighted at the generous way he is treating her in the will.

—So am I.

—Yes indeed. Look, we will have two last drinks for the road. Paddy, two glasses of malt!

—Right, sir.

He brought those deep yellow drinks and placed them before us.

—You know, the brother said, a substantial house and three hundred pounds a year for life is no joke. By God it is no joke.

He carefully put some water in his whiskey.

—Annie is an industrious, well-built, quiet girl. There are not so many of them knocking about. And you don't see many of that decent type across in London. Over there they are nearly all prostitutes.

—Perhaps you don't meet the right people.

—Oh, I meet enough, don't you worry. Decent people are rare everywhere.

I grunted.

—And decent people who are well got are the rarest of all.

—Occasionally decent people get a right dose of Gravid Water.

He ignored this and picked up his drink.

—In my opinion, he said solemnly, half your own battle was won if you decided to settle down. Tell me this much: have you ever had a wish for Annie?

—WHAT . . . ?

He raised the glass of whiskey to his lips and drained it all away in one monstrous gulp. He then slapped me on the shoulder.

—Think about it!

The slam of the door told me he was gone. In a daze I lifted my own glass and without knowing what I was doing did exactly what the brother did, drained the glass in one vast swallow. Then I walked quickly but did not run to the lavatory. There, everything inside me came up in a tidal surge of vomit.

The John F. Byrne Irish Literature Series is made possible through a generous contribution by an anonymous individual. This contribution will allow Dalkey Archive Press to publish one book per year in this series.

Born and raised in Chicago, John F. Byrne was an educator and critic who helped to found the *Review of Contemporary Fiction* and was also an editor for Dalkey Archive Press. Although his primary interest was Victorian literature, he spent much of his career teaching modern literature, especially such Irish writers as James Joyce, Samuel Beckett, and Flann O'Brien. He died in 1998, but his influence on both the *Review* and Dalkey Archive Press will be lasting.

SELECTED DALKEY ARCHIVE PAPERBACKS

FOR A FULL LIST OF PUBLICATIONS, VISIT:

www.dalkeyarchive.com